RIDING THE VENGEANCE TRAIL

Thomas Fury had a young wife, a child on the way, and a farm to tend. They had kept him busy; but he'd enjoyed the toil, for he knew that he was building a future for himself and his family. That future, though, was shattered one afternoon when five riders, led by Luke Marlow, blew in. Soon gunshots rang out, and Thomas Fury's world fell apart. Now Fury rides the vengeance trail, driven on by a desire to deal out justice to those who have destroyed everything that mattered to him . . .

JACK MARTIN

RIDING THE VENGEANCE TRAIL

Complete and Unabridged

LINFORD
Leicester

First published in Great Britain in 2016 by
Robert Hale
an imprint of The Crowood Press
Wiltshire

First Linford Edition
published 2019
by arrangement with
The Crowood Press
Wiltshire

A catalogue record for this book is available
from the British Library.

ISBN 978–1–4448–4142–8

Published by
F. A. Thorpe (Publishing)
Anstey, Leicestershire

Set by Words & Graphics Ltd.
Anstey, Leicestershire
Printed and bound in Great Britain by
T. J. International Ltd., Padstow, Cornwall

This book is printed on acid-free paper

This book is dedicated to my fellow
Black Horse riders, who keep the
spirit of the West alive.

And in memory of Randy Johnson,
fan and friend.

'Revenge, the sweetest morsel to the mouth that ever was cooked in hell.'
Sir Walter Scott, The Heart of Mid-Lothian

1

'Gutless is what you are,' Jim Tanner yelled and crossed the room, peered through the slats at the window and then turned back to his son. He shook his head and ran a hand over the stubble on his chin. 'You craven bastard.'

Ethan glared back at his father, holding the older man's eyes with his gaze. 'I ain't no coward,' he said. 'Just not a damn fool is all. If I go out there Fury'll shoot me down. I'll have no chance. That ain't cowardly, that's just good sense.'

'Pity you didn't show that good sense when you started all this,' Jim said and bit the end off a large cigar. He spat tobacco onto the floor, earning himself a look of reproach from his wife who sat in the far corner, a worried expression permanently plastered across her once beautiful face. She could tolerate her husband's cussing but his vile habit of spitting was best done out of doors.

'You and your damn fool friends started all this,' Jim sucked the cigar to life, and released a fragrant cloud of smoke into the air. 'Why, I should simply throw you out there to face Fury.'

'That's man's an animal,' Ethan said and tried to stop his hands from shaking. 'He ain't no ordinary man. That son of a bitch just won't take killing.'

'Don't see anything,' Jim said, ignoring his son while he once again peered through the window slats. Only a moment ago, Fury had announced his presence by yelling for Ethan to come out and face him and yet he was nowhere to be seen. It was too damn dark to see more than a few feet and the old man could make out nothing but the vaguest of shapes, none of them looking even remotely like a man.

'I ain't going out there, Pa,' Ethan said, firmly.

Jim again peered through the window slats. He held the rifle tightly in his hands and cursed beneath his breath. It was a dark night, absolutely no moonlight; not a star visible in the overcast Arizona sky.

'Send the boy out,' Fury yelled. Jim couldn't make out exactly where the voice had come from. It was as if the world ended a few feet from the ranch house, swallowed up by an inky blackness.

'He'll come out,' Jim yelled back. 'But not for you. He'll come out for the law.'

'The law ain't concerned with this,' Fury yelled back. 'Send the boy out and you can go in peace. I ain't got no argument with you.'

'You killed a lawman's son,' Jim shouted, eyes frantically scanning the darkness for any sign of Fury. The man had to be somewhere.

'I did,' Fury retorted, matter of factly.

'Cole Thornton,' Jim said. 'You gunned him down. Shot him in the back of the head, I hear.'

'That weren't exactly the way it played out,' Fury shouted and then added, 'But I killed him sure enough. Now send the boy out.'

'Ain't there been enough killing?'

'Not near enough,' Fury retorted.

'He's my son,' Jim yelled back. 'You can't expect me to send him out to certain death. If you've got an argument with my boy then I'll make it my argument.'

'Fair enough,' Fury replied.

'Then leave us in peace,' Jim yelled back. 'You have my word I'll take my boy to face the law myself. There'll be a fair trial. That's the only way to end this.'

'Ain't the only way,' Fury retorted. 'You going to send the boy out or ain't you going to send him out?'

'I ain't.'

'Fair enough.'

Suddenly there was a flash and the

simultaneous roar of a high-powered rifle.

Jim was thrown back from the now ruined window; shards of glass, wood splinters and specks of blood seeming to hang suspended in the air. He crashed into the table and slid to the floor. He didn't utter a word but groaned post mortem as air escaped his lungs. The top of his head had been taken clean off, brain matter and skull fragments mixed in with the blood. The bullet had hit him in the side of the head, pulping one eye, had torn through soft matter, mushroomed when it hit the hard bone of the man's skull and then exited with a gush of blood, brains and ruined cranium.

The man's wife screamed.

Ethan looked first at his mother and then at his father's body. He ran to his father and snatched the rifle from the floor where it had landed after sliding from the dead man's hands. There was gore on the stock and the boy rubbed it off and then looked at the blood on his own hands. His father's blood.

Ethan knew that this was his fault; deep down he knew that, but Ethan had never been one to take responsibility for his own actions and he screamed out in both anger and anguish, 'FURY!'

What did Fury have to go and do that for? This was nothing to do with the old man. All the old man had been doing was trying to protect his son, his own flesh and blood — you couldn't blame a man for that.

Fury should have understood that. After all, this was all about flesh and blood.

'I'm going out there,' he said but his mother didn't hear him and she slid from her own chair, crawled to her husband's body and cradled the gruesome mess that was his head in her lap. Blood stained her flowered pinny. Once again she screamed, a yell that increased in intensity before reaching a cutting-off point and then subsiding to a plaintive sob.

'He killed your pa,' she said, as

though not believing it. 'He killed your pa. Shot him dead. Ethan, your pa's dead. Dead.'

Ethan nodded.

'He'll kill you too.' The old woman shook her head, a cold despair had fallen over her, covering her like a burial shroud. She locked eyes with her son, a distant look crossed her face and then she said, simply and without emotion, 'I guess you deserve killing for what you've done. I guess in a way it was you that killed your own father.'

'Don't talk like that, Ma,' Ethan said, his tone plaintive.

The old woman shook her head.

'It was you that did this,' she said, cradling her dead husband's head. She was oblivious to the thick gore that was all over her hands and clothes. 'It was you who brought this man here. You.'

Ethan took one last at his father and then ran to the door, released the bolt and kicked it open. He stood there for a moment in the doorway, silhouetted against the bright interior of the house, before taking a step outside into a night that was blacker than any night had a right to be.

'Ethan Tanner,' Fury's voice came from the left and Ethan turned, fired blindly and heard the shot ricochet off a rock. 'You know why I'm here.'

'Yes, dammit,' Ethan said. 'I know why you're here, you bastard. Show yourself.'

Then Fury stepped out of concealment and stood there, not more than ten feet away from Ethan. His hands hung loose by his sides, the butts of his twin Colts, facing forward, were plainly visible in their holsters. His rifle was in a pouch, slung over his back so that the stock protruded over his left shoulder. He was dressed almost entirely in black; even the Stetson perched at a jaunty angle atop his head was black, the only variation in colour being the off-white of his shirt and the charcoal grey of his hatband. He stood there staring at Ethan, his pale blue eyes appeared grey in the poor light and his sun-hardened skin had the appearance of aged leather.

'You killed my pa,' Ethan said.

'Reckon so,' Fury replied, spat on the ground. 'I warned the old man. He took no heed of those warnings.'

'You killed him,' Ethan said again.

'Kin for kin, I guess you could say.' Fury smiled. It was a cold smile; rictus.

'Son of a bitch,' Ethan said and lifted his rifle but he hadn't even aimed the gun before Fury cleared leather and blew a hole in the centre of his chest. Ethan was lifted from his feet with the power of the blast and thrown backwards. The wall of the house stopped him and he slid to the ground, his blood seeping into the dirt, his eyes staring sightlessly at the man who had taken his life.

'Kin for kin,' Fury repeated and holstered his weapon.

The old woman appeared in the doorway. She was sobbing, her eyes wide in shock and grief and in her hands she held a scattergun that her husband had sawn off to make it more manoeuvrable for quick firing.

'Best you put that cannon down,' Fury warned, with little emotion in his voice. His eyes were unblinking as he stared at the old woman.

'You killed my husband,' the old woman said, between sobs. 'You killed my son too.'

'Reckon so,' Fury said. Again his words were cold and delivered without any emotion whatsoever. 'I told your husband to send the boy out. All I wanted was the boy but he wouldn't listen. Still, reckon I would have done the same in your husband's position.'

'You dirty bastard,' the old woman screamed, perhaps cussing for the first time in her life.

Fury nodded, said, 'Guess you've got the measure of me, lady.'

'Dirty bastard,' the old woman repeated.

'We've established that fact,' Fury replied. 'Now put that big old gun down. It must be feeling pretty heavy in your dainty little hands.'

'You've taken everything,' the old woman said. 'I've got nothing left now. I'm all alone.'

'Ain't nice to lose everything,' Fury agreed. 'Ain't nice at all.'

For a moment it looked as though the old woman was going to fire the shotgun but then she dropped it, allowed it to fall to the ground and collapsed to her knees. She let out a hysterical scream before burying her face in her hands and falling silent.

Fury watched her for a moment. His own face was expressionless, cold.

The old woman remained there on the ground, her body shaking, but she didn't utter another word.

'Tell the others I'm coming for them,' Fury said and calmly turned away.

The old woman reached out and lifted the shotgun, putting it to her shoulder and taking aim at the retreating man's back.

Fury spun on his feet, clearing leather as he did so, and held his gun aimed squarely at the old woman.

'I sure don't want to kill you,' he said. 'Don't make me. That's what your husband did and look what happened to him.'

For several long moments, the woman held the shotgun levelled at Fury. A look of confusion crossed her face and she finally lowered the gun and bowed her head, her shoulders animated with her sobs.

'Kin for kin,' Fury said again and holstered his Colt.

Moments later he rode away, not looking back until he was once again swallowed up by the night.

Fury felt at home in the night.

2

'Fury's killed Ethan Tanner,' Griz said. 'He killed his pa too, shot down the old man.'

'When?'

'Three days past,' Griz scratched his chin. 'The sheriff heard this morning and immediately sent his deputy with the message.'

Wearily, Dan Marlow looked up from his paperwork and sighed. He removed the wire-rim spectacles he wore and massaged the bridge of his nose. He leaned back in his chair and closed his eyes, cursing Thomas Fury.

'I've got men out everywhere looking for Fury,' he said. 'I've got bounty killers and the law on his tail and yet he simply walks into the Tanner place and guns down the boy and his father.'

Griz nodded, said nothing.

'You say the deputy's here now?' Marlow asked.

'Yeah, Steve Carter. Ellie's making him coffee and breakfast before he rides back to town.' Carter was a fresh-faced deputy, only just into his twenties and carrying a blazing torch for Ellie Marlow. No doubt being sent out to the Marlow ranch with the news was the highlight of his day.

'Ride into Sand Creek with the deputy,' Marlow said. 'Get the sheriff out here. If he grumbles tell him I'm ordering that he move his fat useless ass. I need to see him and not some hired hand of a deputy who spends all his time mooning over my daughter.'

Griz nodded, again said nothing and turned on his feet.

Once he was alone, Marlow crossed the room and went to the cabinet he'd had shipped over from one of New York's finest stores. The cabinet had been constructed in London by master craftsmen, and was a thing of beauty, gleaming teak doors with silver handles and when you opened the doors you were greeted with a set of stained glass shelves, all well stocked with both liquor and various wines. Marlow didn't tend to drink in the day — well, except for the occasional glass of wine with his afternoon meal — but today he reached for the whiskey and poured a generous measure into a crystal glass tumbler.

Right about now he needed a stiff drink.

Fury was getting closer and although Marlow had been half expecting this, he had been hoping that Fury would simply vanish, but a month ago Fury had walked into a saloon in Cougar Town and shot Cole Thornton through the back of the head. He'd identified himself to the witnesses, and there were several, as Thomas Fury, telling them that he was on the vengeance trail and to put the word about. He wanted word to spread, so that those he was looking for would know that he was coming for them. And now three days ago he'd gotten Ethan Tanner, which left only the Billings boys and Marlow's own son, Luke. Cole Thornton had been the son of the sheriff of Cougar Town but Fury had simply gunned him down and then left town without breaking a sweat.

Marlow drained the whiskey, poured another, opened one of the drawers in the cabinet and pulled out his small Derringer, then dropped it into the pocket of his housecoat. From now on and until Fury lay dead in the dirt, until he'd seen the man's corpse with his own eyes, he would be armed. Day and night he would have some sort of weapon on him.

It was highly unlikely that Fury would be able to get anywhere near the ranch, they were too well fortified for that. Not only was the ranch situated in a natural valley, surrounded by towering, almost impassable cliffs but there were a lot of men around the place, far too many for Fury to get through. With a little bit of planning the ranch could be turned into a fortress capable of withstanding an attacking army so they should have little problem with one man on a vengeance trail.

Indeed, Marlow knew how to defend the valley.

Years back, during the worst of the Indian troubles, he had been able to hold off an entire army of Apaches in a battle that had lasted for several hours. Afterwards many of the Indians lay dead but Marlow had lost only two men, and one of those men had actually shot himself in his panic to pull his gun. The bullet had entered the man's groin, obliterating a major artery and blasting his genitals out of existence. Yeah, Marlow knew only too well how to defend the valley, how to turn it into a stronghold that Fury would never penetrate.

That would be the plan, the always-cautious Marlow decided. He'd turn the ranch into a bastion with only one way in and one way out. The entrance to the valley would be guarded day and night by several heavily-armed men, others would be placed around the surrounding cliffs, specially prepared dug-outs would be constructed where men could remain hidden away. For twenty-four hours a day until Fury had been stopped, there would be armed men guarding the entrance to the fertile valley where Marlow had built his home.

After draining his second drink, Marlow left his office and went through to the living room where Ellie was seated, reading a well-thumbed book.

'From now on you don't leave the house without first telling me,' Marlow said. 'And if you go into town you take at least three men with you. And only then with my permission.'

Ellie looked up from the pages of her book, a quizzical expression on her face.

'Father . . . ' she said, but Marlow held up a hand to silence her.

'Don't question my motives,' he said. 'Just do as I say.'

She nodded, smiled meekly and said

with an air of resignation, 'As you wish, Father.'

Marlow didn't say another word and went outside in search of the ranch foreman. Ned Rawlings had been with him for almost as long as he had been here in the valley, and Marlow trusted him like he was his own flesh and blood. There was a time when Rawlings would have been useful in a fight, but he was getting on now; too many years weighed him down for him to be any good as a fighting man. Ned Rawlings though was still the man Marlow turned to when he wanted something done.

Marlow found Ned over by the south corral supervising a bunch of cowboys who were trying to break in a particularly ferocious stallion. He stood there for a few minutes watching a cowboy being tossed about on the beast's back. It looked at one point that the cowboy was going to wear the horse down but just when it seemed as if the beast had run out of sand, it lifted its hind legs, bucking the rider from it and sending him crashing into the dirt. The other men watching laughed and then two of them ran over to help the dazed cowboy to his feet.

'Ned,' Marlow said. 'I'd like to speak to you.'

Ned turned and nodded his head before shouting back to the cowboys.

'Guess that'll do for now, boys. We'll try again tomorrow.'

The cowboys sure seem relieved at that.

'That's one tough horse,' Ned said as he came over to his boss.

'You've broken worse,' Marlow said, complimenting his man.

Ned cast a glance back over his shoulder. 'I guess I have,' he said. 'But that was some time ago now. Back then I didn't used to creak when I walk.'

'Guess we all creak a little,' Marlow said and watched the cowboys carefully leading the stallion into the stables. 'Walk with me a' ways.'

Ned glanced at his boss, knowing

that the look upon his face meant trouble. And given all that was going on, he guessed this would have something to do with Thomas Fury. Ned didn't want to get involved in the Fury problem, and although he would never tell his boss, it was with Fury that his sympathies lay. Those men, boys really, Marlow's son among them, shouldn't have done what they done and the way Ned figured it they had it coming to them.

'Fury's proving a hard kill,' Marlow said as they walked and Ned simply nodded in reply. 'He's gonna come here. I've got no doubt of that and we need to be ready for him.'

'You think he's crazy enough to ride in here?' Ned shook his head. He had heard a lot about Thomas Fury but coming here, with so many guns about, would be nothing short of suicide.

Marlow stopped in his tracks, took a glance over his shoulder and took a thin cigar from the breast pocket of his waistcoat. He took a lucifer to it and savoured the smoke for a moment before answering. 'Fury's crazy enough to come here,' he said. 'I'm sure of it.'

'I'm no gunman,' Ned said, 'if that's what's on your mind. I can pretty much take care of business around here but I ain't going to face Thomas Fury in no gunfight.'

Marlow smiled, allowed a trickle of smoke to escape from the corners of his mouth.

'I know that,' he said. 'But what you are is a damn good foreman. You know how to coordinate the men and I'm going to need every man to know what is expected of him if Fury comes here.' Marlow fell silent for a moment, thoughtful and then corrected himself, 'When Fury gets here.'

'I'll do what I can,' Ned said. 'You know that.'

'I know that,' Marlow nodded. 'Your loyalty is never in question, nor your abilities. Which is why I need to talk to you.'

Marlow told his foreman of his plans

to fortify the valley, and gave him instructions to figure out what supplies they'd need, lumber especially, in order to realise this. Ned listened intently to his boss, thinking that he was turning the valley into a stronghold able to withstand an attacking army. Problem was, they were not expecting an army to attack but rather just one man, and where an army could be seen approaching, Fury seemed to pop up out of thin air.

Marlow spent a half hour talking to his foreman and then made his way back to the ranch house where he poured himself yet another whiskey and sat waiting for the sheriff to arrive. Eventually he started to doze; next thing Marlow knew was Ellie gently shaking him awake.

'Wake up,' she said. 'The sheriff's here to see you.'

Marlow pulled his watch from his pocket and flipped the nacre-encrusted cover open. It was close to six in the evening, which meant that he'd slept for several hours. He ran a hand over his face and frowned. That's what came of drinking whiskey in the afternoon, he supposed.

'Send him through,' he said and lit himself another of his thin cigars.

A moment later the sheriff came in and nodded to Marlow.

'Howdy,' he said.

The lawman was no stranger here and he sat himself down in the chair by the window. From here he had a good view of what was happening outside and the lawman knew that Marlow could be long-winded, when he started in conversation there was often no stopping him, and it was nice to have something to divert his attention.

Ellie hovered in the doorway.

'Shall I make coffee?' she asked.

'Yes, do that,' Marlow barked and then smiled, realising he had been too brusque with his daughter. 'I mean that would be good of you. Please do.'

Ellie smiled at her father, aware that he was under considerable strain and then went through to the kitchen area.

'Fury's getting closer,' Marlow said, blowing a cloud of pungent smoke into the air.

The sheriff nodded, said, 'He's got the luck of the devil, that one.'

'That man is the devil,' Marlow said.

'Seems that way,' the sheriff nodded.

'Question is, Sheriff,' Marlow caught the lawman with a stern look, 'what are you going to do to protect us?'

'I've got men out looking for him, you know that.'

'Don't seem to be doing any good though, do they?'

The lawman shrugged his shoulders. 'Like I said, Fury's got the luck of the devil.'

'Seems to me,' Marlow said, 'you're forgetting who runs this town. I put you into office and I can just as easily replace you. I want Fury dead.'

The sheriff nodded and took his makings from his pocket. He rolled himself a smoke, crossed the room to where Marlow kept a box of lucifers and struck one against his boot. He brought it to his cigarette, shook it out and flicked it into the fireplace.

'I've got bounty killers on his tail,' he said. 'I've got my own men after him. I don't see as there's anything else I can do.'

'If it was your kin in danger,' Marlow said, 'I'm damn sure you'd find something else you could do.'

Sheriff Dan Hoskins went back to his chair and then looked at Marlow. He said nothing; there was nothing he could say. Marlow was a powerful man. Rich men like him often were, as money and power usually went hand in hand. Marlow had come to this area when it had been nothing more than a wilderness and carved out a great empire. He had politicians in his pocket and the law simply didn't apply to him the way it applied to other men.

'What I want you to do,' Marlow said, 'is find me someone who can track Fury down. Raise the bounty on his head. Do whatever you have to do

— but I want Fury dead.'

Ellie came into the room carrying a tray, which held two cups of coffee and a pot of sugar. She smiled at her father and the sheriff and then set the tray down on the small table between the two men. She nodded at them both and then made her exit.

The sheriff helped himself to the coffee, spooned in several sugars, and took a sip before responding.

'Just whom do you have in mind?' he asked.

'You're the lawman,' Marlow said. 'You deal with bounty hunters all the time. I want the best.'

The sheriff looked at Marlow and nodded. 'Maybe I know someone who could do the job,' he said. 'If the price on Fury's head was high enough.'

Marlow leaned forward in his own chair, spoke through a thick cloud of smoke.

'Who?' he asked.

'Haw Tabor,' the sheriff said. 'He's just about the meanest bounty hunter

27

there is, but he's expensive. Very expensive.'

'Bring him to me,' Marlow said. 'I'll pay whatever price it takes to get the job done.'

3

Fury carefully placed the coffeepot on the ground and peered into the darkness. He trusted his senses, and right now he knew something was wrong.

Very wrong.

Had he heard something?

Fury wasn't sure, but all the same something, a sixth sense perhaps, a skill he had developed due to living a life where danger could arrive at any moment, had set his nerves ajangle, and caused the tiny hairs on the back of his neck to stand to attention.

Whatever it was that had caused this feeling of unease, Fury was thankful for it just as he had always been grateful of it. It gave him an edge and with the life he led, that edge often meant the difference between life and death. When a man lost his edge, allowed his guard to fall, bad things tended to happen. He had lost that edge once before and it had proven costly for him: he would never let it happen again.

Fury'd kept a low fire and several scoops of earth killed all but a few embers. He cleared leather, one of his Colts filling a hand and made for the line of trees behind him, leading his horse. He took the horse some ways into the woods and tethered the animal to a tree, before making his way back to his campsite. He stopped at the tree line though, peering once more into the pure blackness of night, ears straining for a sound, anything.

For a moment there was nothing and Fury started to think that his imagination had been running away with him, but then he heard the snort of a horse, followed by the unmistakable sound of twigs snapping beneath a horse's hoofs. Someone was coming and getting pretty darn close. Fury had chosen this place to make camp because of the seclusion it offered and whoever it was out there in the darkness could only be here for one reason.

There were men out looking for Fury and from the sound of it, at least one of those men was about to find him.

Fury checked his position and gently thumbed the hammer back on his weapon. From the direction the rider was coming he would be able to get a clear shot, whilst keeping the protection offered by the tree line. It became a waiting game and Fury listened as the unseen rider came ever closer.

For a moment there was silence. The rider seemed to have stopped and just as Fury was about to come out from hiding, the clomping sound of the horse started again. Fury took a deep breath and waited, knowing that any moment now the rider would be visible.

Several moments passed before Fury caught a glimpse of the lone horseman. At first the horse appeared as little more than a shadow but as it came closer, Fury could make out the figure slumped in the saddle. If this was one of the bounty killers then the man didn't seem to be aware that he had stumbled onto Thomas Fury. Indeed the man didn't seem to be aware of anything, and appeared to be dozing in the saddle, his horse leading the way. The horse stopped then and sniffed the air, likely picking up the scent of Fury's own horse.

'Sit up,' Fury barked, emerging from behind the tree. 'Keep your hands where I can see them.'

His words startled the man on the horse. He came awake with a jolt and fell clean out of the saddle, hitting the ground with a low groan.

Fury walked over to the man and stood over him, directing the cruel eye of his gun at the figure. The man wore a bulky-looking coat, the collars of which were pulled up over his face. At first Fury couldn't make out any of the man's features, but when the figure rolled over and the coat fell open Fury saw that it wasn't a man at all, but a boy.

A scrawny looking kid.

And a half-breed at that.

'What are you doing out here?' Fury asked.

The boy sat up, crossing his arms over his knees and Fury saw that he wasn't wearing a gun, didn't look to be armed with any weapons. The kid looked half asleep and he rubbed his eyes with the heels of his hands.

'How old are you, boy?'

'I'm thirteen,' the boy said and made to stand up but paused, looking uncertainly at the gun aimed on him. Fury took a step backwards, nodded for the kid to stand but kept his gun levelled. As the kid stood up, Fury could see that there was nothing to him beneath that oversized coat. The boy had the olive skin and bold features of an Indian but the blue eyes of a white man.

'Thirteen?' There was doubt in Fury's voice. He looked more like a nine year old.

'Will be next birthday,' the kid said.

'Big difference between twelve and thirteen,' Fury said. 'Where are your folks?'

'I'm alone,' he replied. 'Don't have folks.'

'Got a name, kid?'

'Rake . . . They call me Rake.'

'Damn peculiar name.'

The kid nodded, gave a slight smile.

'Well Rake, what are you doing out here?'

'Have you got anything to eat?' the kid asked, ignoring the question. He regarded Fury with his deep blue eyes.

Fury wondered if the kid could be some sort of decoy, if he had been sent on ahead of a team of bounty hunters in order to trick Fury into relaxing. There could be others out there waiting for the opportunity to rush the camp. All of these thoughts crossed Fury's mind but eventually he holstered his weapon and went back in amongst the trees. A moment later he returned and tossed a piece of jerky to the kid.

34

'What are you doing out here?' Fury asked again.

The kid looked at Fury, said nothing. He tore off a strip of the jerky with his teeth and chewed hungrily, before biting off another strip. He swallowed audibly and Fury tossed him a canteen of water.

The kid gulped down several mouthfuls with a thirst that suggested this was the first drink he'd had in some time.

'I asked what you were doing out here?' Fury took the makings from his shirt and rolled himself a quirly. He took a match to the smoke and regarded the kid. The boy claimed to be twelve years old, almost thirteen but looked even younger. However old he truly was, he was hardly of an age to be riding about during the dead of night, especially not alone and especially not out here.

'Well?' Fury prompted.

The kid took a long look at Fury before answering.

'I killed a man,' he said.

'You killed a man?'

The kid nodded. 'Yeah,' he said. 'I killed him sure enough.'

'Anyone after you?' Fury asked. He couldn't imagine this scrawny looking kid being able to lift a gun, let alone shoot anyone.

'I'm not sure.' The kid shrugged his shoulders. 'I don't think so. Well, I guess I don't rightly know.'

Fury drew on his quirly and nodded.

'I'll get the fire going,' he said. 'Fix us some coffee and get some beans on. You look in need of a meal or two.'

The kid nodded, chewing on the last of the jerky. Right about now beans and coffee sounded damn good to him.

'Then,' Fury said, 'you can tell me all about this man you reckon you killed.'

4

Rake claimed to be part Apache.

His father, he said, had been a white man, a mountain man back when the mountains were still largely unexplored. His mother, a full-blooded Apache. It was his mother's side he favoured. He took great pride in this and told Fury that his mother's bloodline could be traced back many generations, to a time before white men came to these lands. Rake had been told this by his grandfather, a man the boy called Running Stream. He was a great tribal leader, the boy boasted, fiercely proud of his Apache heritage. His grandfather's father, a man he had never known, was the last of his tribe to possess the gift that allowed him to talk in the language of animals, and converse with those in the spirit world. These gifts though, the boy said, had been lost to time and these days no Apache, not even those of pure blood, had the ability.

Fury listened to the kid, sipping his coffee while he did so, but he wasn't really interested in the mystical claptrap and only wanted to know why the boy had been out here alone, wandering aimlessly in the dead of night. He claimed to have killed a man and that was something Fury was deeply interested in. He had enough troubles of his own and didn't want this kid sharing his campfire just to add to them.

'You said you killed a man,' Fury eventually prompted. He'd listened to enough now and wanted to cut to the chase. Since they'd eaten, the kid's tongue had been flapping like a flag in a prairie wind, but he hadn't really said anything of note. It seemed as if he had given Fury the entire history of the Apache people but none of that explained his presence here.

The boy's face clouded over and as he peered into the campfire his eyes seemed to be focusing on something far distant, something that belonged to another place, another time.

'I killed the son of a bitch,' he said again.

'You told me that.' Fury shifted to work a cramp out of a leg and took the pouch he wore tied with a string around his neck and removed his makings. He quickly put together a cigarette. 'What you didn't say is who and why.'

'I don't much like thinking about it,' the kid said.

'You're sharing my campfire,' Fury reminded him as if that gave him the right to the boy's innermost secrets.

The kid nodded. 'I was four or maybe five summers,' he said, 'when my family were killed, butchered. Soldiers did this and I was taken to the white man's reservation where I was schooled in the ways of the Americans. I didn't like it there and I ran away. At first they found me and brought me back but I ran away again and again. Each time I ran away, they would find me and bring me back and I would be punished. But that made no difference and I continued to escape at every opportunity. I think in the end they grew tired of punishing me and so they stopped looking for me.'

The kid fell silent for a moment; his eyes went to the cooking pot besides the fire. There were a few mouthfuls of beans left there and Fury nodded, telling the boy to help himself.

'For many years I drifted from place to place,' he continued, chewing on a mouthful of beans. 'Sometimes I found myself some work. I was cleaning out saloons as a nine year old and driving cattle a year later. The last job I took was in Sedona, working on a big cattle ranch as a ranch hand. The work was hard, the hours long and I liked it there. I would have still been there had not the rancher's daughter took a liking to me.'

'I can see how that would cause a problem,' Fury said. The kid was a half-breed and Fury couldn't imagine any kind of man looking kindly on his daughter taking up with a breed. Fury'd never had a daughter but he could imagine how he would have felt at such an event. The boy, through no fault of his own, an accident of birth, would always be an outsider. Likely shunned by whites and Indians alike and forced to walk a path between the two, not really belonging to either race.

The kid nodded, swallowed the last of the beans.

'She made moves on me,' he said. 'I did not respond and she told lies. She told her father that I had tried to force myself on her, attempted to take the gift between her legs. The gift that should be kept for a future husband.'

Fury rolled another quirly, took a lucifer to it and gazed off into the darkness. There was a sudden chill in the air but he dare not build up the fire, not with so many men out looking for him.

'You killed the rancher?' he asked.

The kid shook his head.

'No,' he said. 'I killed his son and if he were here I'd kill him again.'

Fury looked at the kid, saw his eyes blazing back. Those eyes seemed older than he truly was; those eyes had seen much and held a weariness that belied the boy's youth. Those eyes had lived seemingly far longer than the face in which they sat.

'The rancher ordered me to leave,' Rake explained. 'I don't think he really believed his daughter but all the same he told me to go. I suppose he felt compelled to take his daughter's side, and the way I figured it being told to go was not as bad as it could have been.'

'Seems a fair man to me,' Fury said.

'Some men would have shot me or had me killed in some other way,' Rake nodded. 'No one would have cared about the murder of an Apache half-breed. And so I gathered my few possessions together and left the ranch. The rancher gave me money, wages he said I was owed, and sent me on my way.'

'Seems a fair man,' Fury repeated.

The kid nodded, said, 'He was a good man but his son was a different kind of man altogether. He came after me. He didn't come alone, but brought two other men with him. They caught up with me that first night.'

Once again the boy fell silent, gazed into the fire as if he was trying to recall what had happened. He moved a little closer to the fire and then looked at Fury for a moment before continuing, but no sooner had he started speaking again than he froze as the sound of a rifle cocking sounded.

Fury went for his gun but stopped his play when he heard a click as the hammer of a pistol was thumbed back. A man came into view in front of them while another came from behind. Fury looked at the boy and cursed himself for his stupidity. So the kid had been a decoy all along, sent here to distract Fury while the two men sneaked into the camp.

He had been played for a fool and it looked as if it would cost him his life.

'Very slowly unbuckle your guns,' the man holding the rifle ordered and came closer to Fury. He stood just the other side of the campfire, the flames illuminating his hard features and giving him a demonic appearance. Although Fury didn't turn to look, he was aware that the man's companion was behind him.

Fury did as he was instructed, releasing the clasp and allowing his belt to fall to the ground.

'Kick them towards me,' the man with the rifle ordered.

Again Fury complied, working a foot under the gun belt and kicking it towards the man with the rifle.

'Now sit down with your hands on your head.' This time the voice came from behind Fury and he slowly lowered himself to the ground. These two men were taking no chances and Fury cast a venom-filled glance at the kid. Rake though looked just as surprised and he watched open-mouthed as the two gunmen kept their guns firmly on Fury. His own rifle was slung over his horse — he'd put it there when he'd taken the beans and coffee from his saddlebags — and Fury cursed himself.

'You,' the man with the Colt addressed the kid. 'Drop your guns.'

The kid opened his oversized coat.

'I ain't got no gun,' he said.

'Well, Thomas Fury.' Rifleman frowned at the kid and then turned back to Fury. 'You don't look so tough now.'

Fury said nothing. He was calculating his chances of turning the tables on these gunmen and not liking the conclusions he was coming to. These men were undoubtedly bounty hunters and would know how to use their weapons.

'He looks like a whole lot of money,' the gunman behind Fury said and laughed.

Rifleman laughed at that too, revealing chipped, tobacco-stained teeth.

'He sure does,' he said. 'You know how much you're worth, Fury?'

Fury had a pretty good idea, he'd seen the wanted posters, but he remained silent, his eyes trained firmly on the man with the rifle.

The kid suddenly got to his feet and darted into the trees. The man with the handgun fired off a wild shot but the darkness had soon swallowed the boy and there was nothing left to aim at.

'Let him go,' Rifleman said. 'Didn't say anything about no Indian shit-kicker on the wanted posters. Let's just concentrate on taking Fury in.'

Fury hadn't taken his eyes from the man with the rifle but the fact that the kid had suddenly bolted puzzled him. These men didn't seem to have any connection to the boy, which Fury couldn't understand. When these men had turned up he had been sure that the kid had been a decoy, used to catch him off guard but now he didn't have the faintest idea what was going on. There was no doubt that the boy had distracted him and that if he'd been alone, then these men would have had no chance of getting anywhere near his camp without being detected. But these men didn't seem to know who the kid was.

'Dead or alive the poster said,' the man behind Fury came around to stand next to his companion. 'Seems to me taking him in dead would be the easiest way.' He held a Colt in his hand and pointed it directly at Fury's stomach. They wouldn't risk destroying Fury's face and finding themselves unable to claim the bounty on his head.

'I tend to agree on that,' Rifleman said. 'All we really need to take back is his head.'

The man with the Colt laughed.

'Head'll be no problem at all,' he said. 'We can throw it in a sack and leave the body for the critters. Sure would be a whole lot easier than dragging his body back for the bounty.'

'Don't even need to waste a bullet on shooting him first,' Rifleman said. 'I got me a big old knife that'll cut through his neck like it was nothing at all. I've skinned grizz with that knife and grizz is a lot tougher than any man's throat.'

'Even Thomas Fury,' the man with the Colt said and laughed as if that was the funniest thing he'd ever heard.

Fury looked at both men and smiled, remaining silent. He considered the possibility of suddenly rushing them, hoping to get to at least one of them before a bullet stopped him dead. If he could knock one of the men from his feet then he had a chance to get a gun, maybe even get the other man before he got off a clear shot. It wasn't really a chance, Fury knew that but all the same he'd rather go by a bullet than have his head hacked off. Maybe it would be better to take the chance, no matter how slim, and hope for the best.

'Let's just shoot the bastard,' the man with the Colt said. 'I don't mind hacking his head off but I'd prefer him dead while I do it. I ain't no sadistic son of a bitch.'

It was then that all hell broke loose.

There was a whistling sound and the man holding the Colt suddenly screamed, dropped his gun and raised his hands to his forehead as a stone bounced off his head. Blood trickled between his fingers and he muttered a few garbled phrases and staggered about senseless, trying to keep his feet. His companion, Rifleman, looked confused and he took his attention, and the aim of his rifle, from Fury for a split second, which was all that Fury needed.

Fury took Rifleman's legs from under him and managed to get on top of him. He made a fist and brought it down hard on the man's nose, feeling bone break beneath the blow. Rifleman screamed in pain and suddenly became 'rifle-lessman' as his weapon clattered to the ground.

Delivering another stinging blow to the man's jaw, Fury grabbed the rifle. He lifted it and swung it at the other man and fired, hitting him square in the belly, lifting him off his feet and sending him crashing to the ground, already dead.

Fury stood up, holding the rifle in his hand, looked down at Rifleman and then coldly shot him square in the face. At this range the bullet took his face apart and left a pulpy mess, through which a single eye could be seen.

'Next time you got to shoot,' Fury said, 'don't talk, just shoot.'

The kid emerged out of the night and Fury spun on his feet, holding the rifle at his hip, ready to fire.

'Don't shoot,' the kid said. He grinned and tossed a stone he was holding from one hand to the other. 'Always was a good aim. I can use a stone like most men use a gun.'

Fury looked at the kid. For a moment his face was stern but then his features broke into a tight smile.

'Sticks and stones,' he said. 'Sticks and stones.'

5

'Welcome to Cash City' the sign announced, but Fury and the kid didn't get much of a welcome, and all they saw as they rode down the main street was just another dying town. No doubt the town had sprung up, even thrived for a period, perhaps during the mining boom, but now it was on its last legs. There was another sign further on, nailed to a board that someone had shot up, faded and blowing in the gentle breeze.

'Cheap Town Lots' the sign announced and went on to say that prime lots were available for both residential and business development. 'Hurry!' the sign nagged, claiming that these lots were being sold rapidly from between twenty-five and a hundred dollars.

'Don't seem like much of a town,' Fury said.

Rake nodded, said nothing.

Still Fury wasn't looking for comfort, only somewhere to restock supplies before riding on to Tombstone where he knew he would find the Billings boys. Once they had been dealt with, there would only be one man left and then this would all be over. That man was Luke Marlow and Fury planned on keeping him for last.

For the moment, Fury was content to have the kid tag along with him. He had proved useful up in the hills and Fury had little doubt that the kid had saved his life, but that wasn't the only reason he had agreed to the kid tagging along. There were a lot of men out looking for Fury and he figured the kid would be an asset in scouting out ahead, locating the men Fury was looking for while he remained in hiding.

Last Fury had heard, the Billings boys were working on a ranch in Tombstone and the law there could be particularly tough, so finding his targets before the law laid eyes on him was, he figured, of paramount importance. He figured he could trust the kid. He had chopped the boy's hair with his knife, which made him look less like an Indian.

The kid had olive skin and wouldn't pass for a white man even with his shorter hair, but Fury figured he could pass for a Mexican. Weren't many Mexicans with blue eyes true enough, but it wasn't totally unheard of. There were a lot of Mexicans working the ranches in the area, they often made the best cowboys, and folks were less inclined to attack a Mex on sight than they would be an Indian, even a half-breed.

The kid weren't much use with a gun, and could only hit anything if he was up real close but he could throw a stone or rock, as he had displayed up in the hills, with incredible precision. Those two bounty hunters had discovered that to their cost. The two men had no longer been in need of their weapons and so the kid was now heeled. He'd also found the coat one of the bounty hunters had been wearing to be a better fit than his own ridiculous garment, which had been made for a much larger man.

The fifty dollars the men had been carrying between them would come in mighty handy and so Fury had taken that, giving the kid a ten-dollar bill, which he readily pushed into his own pocket.

The rest they had left for the critters.

'Don't much like the feeling this place gives me,' the kid said as they rode side by side down the main street.

Fury grunted in agreement, but said nothing. The way he figured it there wasn't anything to say on the subject and chat for the sake of it was something that had always irritated him.

They rode down the main street in silence; both glanced up at the building that was the Cash City Hotel. It was a large two-storey building and no doubt had been a thriving concern when the town had been in better health. Next door stood a saloon and Fury briefly considered getting himself a whiskey, but thought better of it. With so many men out looking for him he figured it best to get about his business and get out of town as quickly as possible.

'There,' the kid pointed, shifting in the saddle.

Fury looked and nodded when he saw the general store. The sign on the wind-ravaged board outside the door read 'General Merchants' and boasted of stocking the finest animal feeds as well as luxury items, including scented soaps from New York City.

The kid pulled his ten-dollar bill from his pocket and reached across to hand it to Fury but Fury shook his head, and the bill went back into his pocket.

'I'll go in,' Fury said, feeling a little uneasy to be in a town, even one as quiet as this one. 'You wait outside with the horses. Keep them ready in case we've got to skedaddle out of here.'

The kid nodded, said, 'I know horses. They will run faster under my care.'

'Sure,' Fury said and gently coaxed his horse into a steady trot. Dust spat up from the hard-baked ground below.

Inside the store, Fury found it to be surprisingly well stocked. It was in direct contrast to the outside. Clean and tidy, not a single speck of dust had been allowed to settle anywhere. There were row upon row of shelves lining the walls. The focal point was a large counter that ran the length of the rear wall and when the bell above the front door sounded, a plump man wearing a rawhide apron and puffing on a corncob pipe came through from a rear room.

'What can I get you, stranger?' he asked, clouds of smoke coming out of the bowl of his pipe.

Fury walked up to the counter, tipped his hat and gave a tight smile. His eyes scanned the storekeeper for any signs of agitation but the man looked perfectly calm. Fury guessed he was getting a little too jumpy, what with his face being on so many wanted posters.

'I'm going to be needing a few things,' Fury said. 'Coffee, beans, jerky. I also need some tobacco.'

'I can do you all those things,' the storekeeper said. 'To be perfectly honest the way things are these days I'm grateful for any business I can get.' He didn't remove the pipe from his mouth as he spoke and billows of fragrant smoke punctuated his words.

'Then let's get to it,' Fury said, growing impatient with the chatter. It was clear that the storekeeper considered passing the time of day with his customers was a part of his duties; Fury though just wanted to get his provisions and get the hell out of this decomposing little town. The more time he spent around people, the more chance there was of someone recognising him as Thomas Fury, a man considered an outlaw and fair game for any trigger-happy young gun out to make a name for himself.

Fury was tired of all the killing and wanted to see the end of it. There were three more men who had to die and after that was done, Fury figured he'd be at peace and would vanish, live the rest of his life out up in the mountains, a solitary existence with only nature herself for company.

'I'm all out of Folgers,' the store-keeper said. 'Will Arbuckle's do?'

For a moment Fury was confused, the storekeeper's question had dragged him out of his reverie. He looked at the storekeeper and smiled.

'Coffee,' he said. 'Sure, Arbuckle's will be fine.'

The storekeeper nodded and started measuring out the beans and then transferring them into a grease-proof sack, pulling the drawstring and sealing it.

'Cash City was going to be a railroad town,' the storekeeper grumbled as he poured beans into another greaseproof sack. 'It boomed for a period but when the railroad decided on a different location for its terminal, it went downhill faster than a whore with a dose.' He chuckled to himself at his last remark, removed his pipe and tapped out the dottle into the palm of his hand. He rubbed the ashes into his apron and then took a pouch of tobacco from a pocket and refilled the pipe.

Fury took his makings from the pouch he wore around his neck, and put together a smoke. He struck a lucifer on the counter and sucked the quirly to life.

'I'll be needing some tobacco too,' Fury reminded the storekeeper, speaking through a mouthful of smoke.

'Sure thing.' The storekeeper chuckled once more, lit his pipe and then continued with his business. 'Any particular brand in mind?'

'I'm easy,' Fury said.

'Durham's the most popular,' the storekeeper said. 'Often smoke it myself.'

'I'm easy,' Fury repeated. 'Give me ten pounds.'

The storekeeper nodded and grabbed two of the sacks with the familiar picture of a bull on the label.

The bell above the door sounded again and the storekeeper looked up, smiling as he saw another customer enter. Today was shaping up to be his best in a long while.

Fury turned to the newcomer and couldn't believe his eyes. He reacted immediately by going for his guns, which on reflection was probably not the wisest move to make but the newcomer had taken Fury by surprise and he had acted on instinct with no conscious thought at all. Before he knew it both of his Colts were in his hands as he stared incredulously at the grubby face of Samuel Billings.

Billings looked at Fury. At first he didn't seem to recognise him, but he was startled to see the guns pulled on him. It was then that realisation dawned and his mouth fell open. He looked as if he had seen a ghost.

'Fury,' he said and quickly turned on his feet. Before Fury could react he had vanished through the front door, slamming it closed behind him.

'I'll be back for my items,' Fury told the startled storekeeper and ran off in pursuit of Sam Billings.

Outside the kid still sat his horse and he looked at Fury with puzzlement in his pale blue eyes.

'Which way did he go?' Fury asked. He looked up and down the street but there was no sign of Billings.

'The man who came tearing out a moment ago?' the kid asked as if Fury could have meant anyone else.

Fury nodded. 'Where did he go?'

'There,' the kid said, pointing to an alley that ran between the hotel and the saloon.

Fury tipped his hat to the kid and ran off in pursuit of Billings.

Coming upon Billings like this had taken Fury completely by surprise, but he wasn't going to allow this opportunity to pass. He wondered if the other Billings brother would be here, and he figured there was a good chance he would be. The brothers tended to stick together and if Fury caught up with the two of them today, then only the Marlow boy would be left. Fury's journey down the vengeance trail would be that much closer to being over. He would finally be able to move on and live out the rest of his life, however short it turned out to be. He knew that he would be a wanted man, an outlaw, until the day he died and would have to live each and every day with one eye looking over his shoulder. Fury didn't fear death but he'd be damned if he'd go before he'd taken out his revenge on those five men who had destroyed everything.

The men who had torn his world apart.

He'd already sent two of them to the grave and the remaining three wouldn't be far behind them.

Fury came out of the alley and

looked up and down the street. He saw Billings enter the livery stable at the far end, and he ran towards the building. He ducked low as he went through the double doors, keeping his Colts in his hands, ready to fire immediately he caught sight of Billings. There was a gunshot and the wood in the doorframe splintered as a slug tore into it. Fury dived towards one of the stalls, startling the horse inside, and carefully looked up over wall of the stall. He saw Billings crouched behind a bale of hay and he let off two shots before ducking down back behind cover.

Billings returned fire; one shot went into the wall while the other carved a furrow along the now terrified horse's back. The horse's wound wasn't life threatening but the beast experienced extreme pain and it reared up onto its hind legs, threatening to trample Fury within the confinement of the stall. Fury slapped the horse's rump, sending the creature tearing out onto the street outside.

Billings shot again; another two shots tore into the wall near where Fury was hiding, sending dust and wood splinters into the air.

'What in damnation's — ?' An old man, likely the owner of the livery stable, came through the double doors just as Billings let off another two shots. The old man looked across and saw Fury crouched in the stall, his Colts in his hands, and turned and ran to get help.

The way Fury figured it, Billings only had one shot left in his gun and he stood and fired in his direction, knowing he had no clear target but hoping to provoke Billings into firing his last shot and then rushing him before he had a chance to reload. Immediately, Billings returned fire and Fury hurled himself out of the stall and crossed the stable, jumped up onto the bale of hay and stood looking down on Samuel Billings, who was frantically trying to thumb a cartridge into his Colt.

Fury shook his head and directed one of his own guns directly at Billing's head.

Billings dropped his gun, whimpered, 'I didn't want to do it. It weren't me. I was just there.'

'Too bad,' Fury said and his finger tensed on the trigger.

'Don't do it, mister. We got you covered.'

Keeping his gun trained on the now cowering Billings, Fury took a glance over his shoulder. A tall, thin man held a rifle on him, which Fury recognised as an '81 model Marlin. The gun at this range would do devastating damage to anything it hit. The man wore the tin star of the sheriff's office and two deputies flanked him, each of them holding a gun. Behind them stood the old man who had run off only moments ago and behind him was the kid, looking wide-eyed at the scene unfolding before his eyes.

'They ain't no concern of yours,' Fury said and glared down at Billings.

He knew if he shot Billings he would be shot down himself, likely in the back before he even had a chance to turn back to the sheriff.

Fury heard the sheriff move and then he felt the cold steel as the rifle was pushed against the back of his neck.

'Put your guns down slowly,' the lawman said. 'Anything that happens in this town is my concern.'

Fury was loath to lower his weapon, but he knew that if he took Billings out now then that would be the end of it, and he would never catch up with the other men. He frowned and slowly lowered his gun and then dropped both weapons to the straw-covered floor.

The next thing he knew there was a heavy blow to the back of his head as the sheriff brutally struck him with his rifle stock. Fury's eyes rolled back in their sockets, his legs weakened . . . and then only blackness.

★   ★   ★

'Will this do?' Rake asked, holding out the crumpled ten-dollar bill. It was all the money the kid had but that didn't matter none to him. He was used to riding around without any money, and Fury had stood him a good meal so he guessed this was the least he could do for the man.

The old man snatched the money from the kid and nodded.

'Want me to give any message?' he asked.

The kid looked at the old man and then shook his head.

'Not really,' he said. 'Just tell him I rode on. Take good care of his horse, mind. Ten dollars worth of care.'

'Sure thing, son,' the old man led Fury's horse into the livery stable.

The kid mounted his own horse and turned the beast around, setting off away from town.

The way he figured it, Fury would spend maybe a night in jail before being released but he wasn't going to hang around waiting. That would be too risky for him. If the lawman discovered he had been with Fury then maybe, just maybe, he'd find out about the man he had killed.

The kid wasn't going to hang around town and take that risk; he wasn't going to invite a rope around his neck. The killing had been self defence, the man had attacked him first but he was a half-breed, the man he'd killed had been the son of a powerful rancher and more than that he had been white. The kid had no doubt that they'd hang him for the killing.

6

At the precise moment that Fury slipped away into unconsciousness, and more than fifty miles away, an immaculately dressed man stepped down from the train at the Sand Creek Terminal. The man's name was Haw Tabor and although he had never met Thomas Fury, indeed had never heard of him until a few days ago when the telegram from Sheriff Hoskins had arrived, their paths were destined to cross.

Held tightly in his left hand, Tabor carried a carpetbag, which contained the tools of his trade. The bag housed a Colt Peacemaker, a Colt .36 Navy, a Derringer and the tools needed to keep each weapon in pristine condition. He also carried a Sharps Big Fifty rifle, which was currently slung over his back and held in place by a strap he had designed himself, and worn down low in his gun-belt was a gleaming Colt Paterson. With a 9-inch barrel, the Paterson wasn't intended for any of that quick draw nonsense written about in the newspapers but for deadly accuracy. Tabor knew that a quick draw weren't really worth a damn. In the heat of a fight what truly mattered were nerves of steel, and a steady hand to hit the target.

Tabor noticed the way folk averted their eyes as he walked down the main street but he didn't let that bother him none. With his long black frock coat, black Levi's and boots he knew that many of those who saw him would take him for what he was, a gunslinger. The fact that he had a mean-looking face, with a scar that ran down his left cheek, parting his lips before meeting his chin, made him look all the more sinister. Clamped between his teeth, hanging from the corner of his mouth, was a bent meerschaum pipe, which left a trail of smoke in his wake.

'You,' Tabor said, catching the attention of a small, balding man who was crossing the street in front of him.

The man stopped, looked directly into Tabor's face and smiled meekly. He was evidently nervous and he swallowed audibly.

'Can I help you, stranger?' he asked.

'Sheriff Hoskins,' Tabor said, removed his pipe and regarded the contents of the bowl for a moment before asking, 'Where can I find him?'

'This time of day I'd try the saloon,' the balding man said.

'Where might that be?'

'End of the street,' the bald man pointed. 'Take the left turn and you can't miss it.'

'Obliged,' Tabor said, tipped his hat and placed his pipe back in his mouth before continuing down the street.

The saloon, named the Bull's Head, was a two-storey building with a false front. It was built on stilts and Tabor stepped up onto the wide boardwalk and paused, listening to the laughter and music coming from inside, before pushing through the batwings.

Tabor stood in the doorway for a moment, taking in his surroundings. There was a green baize table in one corner with a faro game going on, while men sat around drinking, sharing tall tales and laughing. A troop of saloon girls worked the tables, expertly gliding between them, stopping for a moment to give a lonely old cowboy a tempting smile before moving onto the next table and the next lonely cowboy. Tabor watched as one man grabbed one of the girls by the waist and pulled her onto his lap. He tried to kiss her but the girl pulled away until the man pulled several coins from his breast pocket and handed them over. Then the girl immediately fell in love with the cowboy. She kissed him right back and the man whooped out his delight and buried one of his hands in the girl's crotch.

'That's extra,' Tabor heard the girl snap as she pulled away, love being a fickle thing. The cowboy laughed and immediately produced more money.

In the far corner a pianist plunked away at the keys, hardly holding a tune, which was not surprising given the amount of empty beer glasses that rested on top of the brightly polished piano, but no one seemed to mind and the pianist swayed on his stool as he beat out random notes and chords into a melody that was passable, but only barely.

Tabor walked towards the bar, scanning the crowd for the flash of a tin star but the place was packed and he couldn't pick out the sheriff. If the saloon did brisk business like this on a daily basis then the owner, whoever he was, would end up a wealthy man.

It was certainly one of the most fancy saloons Tabor had ever been in; why, it was prettier than most of the whores currently hip-snaking from customer to customer. The floor beneath his feet was tiled and the bar looked to be mahogany while above it a row of mirrors reflected whiskey and brandy bottles. At each end of the bar, Tabor noticed spittoons that looked to be made from solid brass. There was a sign above the bar that read 'Open 24 Hours', and below that was a list of the most popular beverages with names like Tarantula Juice and Skull Crusher.

Tabor had to push two drunken cowboys aside to get to the bar and when one of the men made as if to go for his gun, Tabor pulled open his frock coat, revealing his own gun, and shook his head.

'You don't want to make a play with me,' he warned.

The cowboy seemed to agree and he shrugged his shoulders and laughed.

'Can I get you a drink, stranger?' he asked.

Tabor shook his head, said, 'I'll pay my own way.' And with that he tossed a coin on the bar and stood waiting for the barkeep to attend to him. The cowboy again looked aggrieved, but then he simply took his drink and found himself somewhere to sit that was a goodly distance from the black-garbed gunslinger.

'Whiskey,' Tabor said as the barkeep turned up. 'The good stuff and then you can tell me where I can find the sheriff.'

'Right here,' Sheriff Hoskins said, who was standing at the bar a few men down from Tabor. He pushed the men at the bar aside and went and stood next to the newcomer. 'You Haw Tabor?'

Tabor nodded, looked at the sheriff and thought this weren't much of a lawman. For a start, he was overweight and there was a strong smell of whiskey on his breath. He had a few days of stubble on his chin and his teeth were the colour of faded rope. In short, the man looked a mess.

'I've been waiting for you,' the sheriff said.

'That figures,' Tabor said and produced the telegram from his pocket. 'Since it was you sent this.'

The sheriff nodded and smiled.

'Since you've come,' he said, 'I guess you're gonna' take the job.'

'Business sours the taste of good whiskey,' Tabor said. 'I'll finish my drink and then we'll talk business.'

The sheriff watched as Tabor turned away from him and directed his attention to the amber liquid in the glass the barkeep had served up. He spent several moments peering deep into the heart of the liquid, as if he could see something that others couldn't within the intoxicating swirl of the whiskey. The gunman then removed his pipe, tapped the spent ashes onto the bar and placed it into his breast pocket.

The sheriff shrugged, told the barkeep to set him up another drink and stood waiting for Tabor who sipped his own drink, savouring the taste, seemingly in no hurry to finish. Eventually he finished his drink and then turned to the sheriff, who was also nursing an empty glass.

'Let's talk business,' he said, removing his pipe from his pocket and thumbed tobacco into the bowl.

'My office,' the sheriff said.

'Lead the way.' Tabor stood and followed the lawman out of the saloon.

★ ★ ★

'Mr Marlow'll pay you another five thousand on top of the reward money,' Sheriff Hoskins said. 'That'll make taking Fury down mighty lucrative.'

Tabor examined the wanted poster, taking in every detail of Fury's features from the sketch.

'I don't bring no one in alive,' Tabor said. 'Too much trouble that way.'

'We're aware of that,' the sheriff said. 'Likely that's why you're being offered the job. I think Mr Marlow will sleep a whole lot better knowing Fury's beneath the dirt.'

Tabor carefully folded the wanted poster and put it into the deep breast pocket of his frock coat. He stood and reached out a hand to the sheriff and the two men shook on the deal.

'I'd like to meet this Mr Marlow,' Tabor said, speaking around his ever present pipe.

'There's no need,' the sheriff said. 'I'm acting on behalf of Mr Marlow.'

'All the same,' Tabor said. 'I'd like to see the man face to face before I take the job. Just so there's no misunderstandings.'

The sheriff looked at Tabor and realised it was futile to protest further. He had no doubt that Tabor would catch up with Fury soon and that could only go one way. Fury had been lucky so far, but then the men he'd killed had been nothing more than cowboys. Tabor was a different kind of man altogether, a professional killer, an expert tracker. His name was feared across the West and if any man could be guaranteed to get the job done, then Haw Tabor was such a man.

'Mr Marlow asked me to take care of

business,' the sheriff said and awkwardly scratched at the stubble on his chin.

'I said I'd like to meet him,' Tabor said, his features momentarily lost behind the cloud of smoke that emerged from the large bowl of his pipe.

'Guess you're insisting on that.'

'Guess so,' Tabor said, sending out another thick cloud of smoke.

The sheriff nodded, asked, 'You want to ride out to Marlow's place now or do you maybe want to get some food first?'

'No time like the present,' Tabor said. 'I'll need to get me a horse, though.'

'We can borrow one from the livery stable,' the sheriff said. 'I know the owner and he owes me a few favours.'

'I'd prefer to buy one,' Tabor said. 'A good horse is important in my business and I don't want to be riding around on some lame nag.'

'With the money you're getting for this job, you can sure enough afford a damn good horse,' the sheriff said.

'You know where I can get such a beast?'

'Sure,' the sheriff said.

7

When Fury regained consciousness, he found himself lying on a cold, hard floor. He shook his head, trying to recall what had happened and then felt himself retching. Ignoring the pounding in his head, he managed to get onto all fours and promptly vomited over the cell floor.

'I ain't cleaning that.'

Fury rubbed a hand across his mouth and looked through the bars at the sheriff who was leaning back in his seat, his legs up on his desk, a large cigar clamped between his teeth.

Fury felt the back of his head and found a large lump, tender to the touch. There was also dried blood encrusted in his hair.

'Did you have to hit me quite so hard?' he asked.

'You would have killed that fella if I

hadn't,' the sheriff replied. 'Now what was all that about? I'm debating what to do with you two fellas. I won't have any trouble in my town and the town finance committee won't stand for you being locked up indefinitely.'

Fury looked across into the next cell and there, sat on the bunk, a miserable look upon his face, was Sam Billings. He regarded Fury coldly but soon looked away, not liking what he saw in the other man's eyes.

'Course,' the sheriff continued, 'if I'd just stood back and let you shoot the other fella we could have hung you. Hanging ain't expensive. Plenty of old rope available.' The sheriff chuckled to himself, sending out plumes of smoke from his cigar as he did so.

Fury stood up and went to the wall dividing his cell from the next and held onto the bars. He leaned forward, once again locking his gaze on Billings.

'Why don't you ask him what this is all about?' Fury asked.

The sheriff took his feet from his

desk, his chair coming forward with a crashing sound onto the tiled floor and stood up. He stretched to work a kink out of his back and regarded Billings.

'Want to enlighten me, boy?' the lawman asked.

Billings looked at the sheriff and then at Fury but he said nothing. The lawman thought that the expression upon the man's face brought to mind that of a startled animal.

Fury looked at the lawman and shook his head. He noticed several wanted posters on the wall behind the lawman and was relieved to see that none of them held his likeness. There were papers out on him, but thankfully none seemed to have reached this decomposing little backwater.

'I have my reasons for wanting this man dead,' Fury said. 'I'm going to see he ends up that way.'

'You ain't in any position to do anything about anything,' the lawman said and then scraped the butt of one of his Colts along the bars of the cells, as if to emphasise his point. He holstered his weapon and shook his head. 'Damn, what am I to do with you two?'

'Let us go,' Fury suggested, knowing the lawman wouldn't see that as an option. 'We're going to come face to face eventually. One day there'll be a reckoning and it might as well be today.'

'Release you.' The sheriff looked at Fury and the corners of his mouth formed into a tight smile. 'Why, that's just what I intend to do.'

Billings stared at the lawman, fear clouding his features. He kept his gaze away from Fury but he knew the other man was staring at him, could sense it, almost feel Fury's eyes locked on him.

'See,' the lawman said, 'the way I see it is you two ain't done anything wrong, other than one of you tried to kill the other which don't really concern me except you brought this to my town. Now I can see there's history behind this problem but seeing as neither of you seem to want to tell me just what that is, then I guess it ain't none of my concern. I sure won't lose sleep over it and that much's for certain.'

The sheriff drew hard on his cigar and remained silent for several moments, before, 'I threw you two in here to keep the peace and I sure don't intend to waste town money keeping you in here for any longer than necessary. Nope, not one moment longer than is absolutely necessary. Now the way I see it getting rid of you two as quickly as possible is in the town's best interests.'

'Couldn't agree more,' Fury said.

The sheriff took the keys from the pocket in his waistcoat and went and unlocked Billings cell.

'Step out,' the lawman said and when Billings seemed reticent to do so, he pulled a Colt from his holster. 'Get out here,' he ordered. 'Ain't never had to shoot a man for refusing to leave the cells before but there's always a first time.'

Billings looked for a moment at Fury

and then quickly looked away.

'I won't ask you again,' the lawman prompted.

Billings walked on feet that had suddenly become leaden. He stepped out of the cell and the sheriff swung the door closed.

'He'll kill me,' Billings said, a plaintive quality to his voice.

'That's what I figure,' the lawman said and then yelled for his deputy to 'Get in here'.

Almost immediately the front door opened and a younger man, also wearing a tin star, came in. He had obviously been standing sentry outside the lawman's office.

'This is Tom Ryker,' the lawman said, speaking directly to Billings. 'Tom's my deputy.'

'Howdy,' the deputy said and received a frown from the sheriff. He shrugged his shoulders, apologetically.

'Now he may look to be as effective as a fart in a storm but Tom can handle himself. Least he knows one end of a gun from the other,' the sheriff said, obviously thinking himself a bit of a joker. 'Tom's gonna escort you to the town boundary and see to it that you keep right on going. Don't ever show your face in Cash City. We don't need your sort around here.'

Fury shook the bars of his cell.

'What about me?' he asked.

'Oh I'll be letting you go too,' the sheriff said. 'Though not until this piece of scum is long gone.' He pointed at Billings with his Colt. 'You want to kill him, you can chase him down and do your killing someplace else.'

Billings sighed, suddenly feeling a lot more relaxed. He was being given a chance to get away from Fury and that was not an opportunity he'd ignore. The sheriff didn't need to make it clear about not returning to Cash City. Billings had no intention of ever coming back. He cast another glance at Fury and immediately looked away again, as if burned by the hate coming from the other man's eyes.

The sheriff crossed the room and took Billings' rig down from the pin on the wall. He examined the gun for a moment, the butt scuffed where it had been used to hammer down on something, likely a nail. It wasn't the way to treat a weapon and the sheriff shook his head before tossing the gun belt to his deputy.

'Don't give him his weapon until you reach the town border,' the lawman ordered and then addressed himself directly to Billings, 'Remember, I don't ever want to see you around these parts again.'

Billings nodded, eager to be on his way, to get as far away from Fury as possible. He planned on riding out, going directly to his brother who was camped just outside town with the herd they were working, and then moving on before Fury tracked them down. Fury had already killed three men since setting out on his vengeance trail, least ways there were three that Billings knew about and it was likely there were more.

'Get him out of here,' the sheriff barked and watched the deputy lead the man out of the office.

'You've done me a disservice, lawman,' Fury said and sat back onto his bunk.

'Sure,' the sheriff said and went and sat back behind his desk. 'And don't my heart just grieve over that fact.'

Fury closed his eyes, cursing the fact that he had chanced upon Billings like this and yet failed to kill him. He should have shot Billings immediately he'd seen him, but he had been taken by surprise. Billings had been the last man he'd expected to see walking into the store and Fury knew that he had reacted too slowly, that his amazement at seeing the man walking in like that had gotten the better of him.

Damn fool, Fury chided himself.

If only he'd acted quicker, shot Billings where he'd stood then he could have been long gone before the portly sheriff had arrived on the scene. Still, there was nothing that could be done at the moment, and Fury realized it was futile to torture himself with 'what if' and 'maybe'. The lawman wouldn't release him until he was good and ready to do so and that was the truth of it.

Thinking these thoughts, Fury drifted off into an uneasy sleep and once again the memories returned to torment him. They were always there, hidden away in the back of his mind only to come forth whenever he allowed himself the luxury of sleep. Fury understood that the memories would be played out over and over, night after night and only by killing those men would he ever find peace. Until then the memories would steal all benefit from his sleep, bring him awake, sweat soaked and sobbing. Until he had taken the final step of his vengeance trail Fury would never be able to move on. Those memories would always be there, would never truly be vanquished from his mind, but only when the last man died would he be able to have some semblance of a life.

Not that Fury cared what happened

after he had killed the last of the men he had vowed vengeance upon.

For now vengeance was all he lived for and once that had been obtained . . . well, Fury didn't much care what happened after that.

Now, though, as he dozed Fury entered a world gone by, though imprinted forever upon his memory.

Fury once again relived the events that had started all this.

He had been working the fields when he'd seen the distant riders approaching, five of them. They rode in tight formation, almost like a military troop and Fury cursed when he realised the riders intended stopping at the house, likely they would expect to rest their horses and maybe get a meal. There were great distances between here and the next town and Fury knew that it would be expected of him to provide nourishment to the riders, to welcome them to share the little he had. Hospitality would be expected; such was the way of things out here on the frontier.

Fury saw his wife come out of the house and he quickly made his way across the fields. The riders were still some ways off and Fury knew that he would reach the house before they did, which was just as well since he wasn't wearing a gun. And hospitality or not, he intended to be careful until he knew what intent the riders carried in their hearts. He reached the house, smiled at his wife and then went inside and emerged a moment later carrying his rifle. Noticing his wife's eyes when she saw the gun, he placed a reassuring hand on her shoulder.

'Everything'll be fine,' he said.

His wife smiled back at him. It was a smile that Fury never tired of, and he guessed he never would. Her eyes seemed to sparkle, almost like precious stones when she smiled. Fury smiled back, looking at her midriff, just as he did several times a day, to see if she was showing yet but it was early days and there was no real visible sign of her pregnancy.

'Likely drifters,' Fury said. 'Lots of men moving around at the moment, searching for opportunities, a way to make a mark.'

Rose nodded and placed an arm around her husband's waist.

'Just as we have here,' she said.

'Yeah,' Fury agreed, thinking that the spread may not be much at the moment but given time he knew he could turn this place into something they could be proud of. Rose was with child and Fury was certain it was a son she carried.

'Shall I put some coffee on the stove?' Rose asked.

Fury nodded, not taking his eyes from the approaching riders.

When Rose was inside, Fury crossed to the fence that enclosed his wife's vegetable garden, and keeping his rifle pointed at the ground he waved a hand to the riders and smiled when one of them waved back.

'Hello there,' he shouted. 'You're welcome.'

Though Fury still felt uneasy at the fact that there were five of them and only one of him. If they planned on doing any harm then he had to be ready if he was to have any chance of protecting what was his. These days it paid to be careful, especially out here on the frontier where the only law for miles around was the law of the gun.

As the riders grew closer, Fury immediately recognised the lead rider as Luke Marlow. The Marlow family were well known and owned a large spread of land a couple of days' ride distant. Dan Marlow, Luke's father, had founded the town of Sand Creek, erecting the first buildings when there had been nothing but wilderness for many miles around and from there the town had grown, as had Marlow's standing and influence. Fury had met Dan Marlow several times, had even purchased some stock from his ranch but he hadn't much liked the man. Like many wealthy men who had made their considerable wealth from nothing, he had been arrogant, seemed to think himself a touch above most other folk, especially a poor cowboy with a young family like Thomas Fury. The Marlow empire had been founded on cattle; during the war Marlow had made a fortune supplying meat to the army and since then he'd gained lucrative railroad contracts which had allowed him to buy out a long-abandoned Arizona silver mine that many believed to have been worked out, but under Marlow's supervision had yielded considerable wealth. Indeed the mine continued to do so and the Marlow Mining Company, its MMC logo looking like a cattle brand, was a name known across the country.

'Mr Marlow,' Fury said as the riders came upon the ranch. 'You and your men and most welcome to enjoy a meal from our table.'

'Obliged,' Marlow said and dismounted. He tethered his horse to the fence that contained Rose's vegetable patch and the rest of his men did likewise.

Fury looked at Marlow's companions and recognised the two Billings boys but he didn't know the others. The Billings, Sam and Deke, were wandering cowhands who hired themselves onto whatever outfits were looking for men and Fury figured that they were currently working for Marlow's outfit. He had served alongside the brothers during the war, but it had been more than five years since the war had ended and he'd not seen them since they'd discarded the grey uniform. As Fury recalled, the Billings boys ain't been much at soldiering, had been lazy, insubordinate and often cowardly. There had been many men like these during the war, men who had somehow survived the terrible years of battle while other, far better men, had not.

'Where you fellas heading?' Fury asked.

'Home,' Marlow said and pushed past Fury as if he had a right to be there. He was heading towards the house and Fury quickly moved in front of him.

'You men are welcome to wash up and water your horses,' Fury said. 'Then I hope you'll partake in a meal before moving on.'

Fury didn't like the way Marlow's companions were standing around, hands poised as though ready to pull iron as they watched the exchange between Fury and their leader. It was then that Rose came back out of the house, carrying a tray of fresh bread, which she took over to the small table her husband had built so they could take supper while watching the sunset. The Arizona sunsets were often vivid and always a sight to behold.

'I've got enough stew for everyone,' Rose said and smiled at her husband.

Fury didn't like the way Marlow's eyes were taking in his wife, but he said nothing and instead gestured towards the table with his rifle. There were long benches each side of the table.

Marlow locked eyes with Fury for a moment but then smiled and removed his hat. He turned back to his men.

'Come on, men,' he said, taking a place at the table. 'You heard these good people. There's a mighty tasty meal waiting for us.'

Fury felt himself relax as he saw the other men take up places around the table. He had originally built the table for him and Rose to share, but he had been looking towards the future and a family and the table was big enough to accommodate the five men with comfort. In fact there was room for another couple of people. Thomas Fury had intended to be mighty busy with the family-making business.

Rose came out of the house again and placed a steaming coffee pot on the table. 'I'll get cups,' she said and Fury once again noticed that Marlow's eyes were taking a journey over his wife's body.

'I'll help you,' Fury said, leaned his rifle against the wall and followed his wife into the house.

One inside, Fury grabbed his wife by one of her arms and turned her to face him.

'Just serve the food,' he said, 'and come back inside.'

'You worried about these men?' Rose asked, reading the concern in her husband's eyes.

Fury bit his lower lip in concentration.

'I'll feel a whole lot easier when they ride on,' he said and gently kissed his wife before turning to go back to the men. He reached the doorway, put one step outside and then the world exploded around him. He felt the red heat of a slug tearing into his side, and he was thrown into the air. He hit the ground and it was only then that he heard the sound of the gunshot. The bullet had torn into his side and was the worse agony Fury had ever felt. He tried to get to his feet, but couldn't. Nor could he speak and hot blood bubbled over his lips.

Blackness came and took him but just before Fury slipped into unconsciousness he heard Rose scream and then . . . then nothing.

★   ★   ★

Fury opened his eyes and stared up at the roof of his cell. He breathed in deeply while the final residues of the memory drifted from his mind.

The sheriff was sat back, reclining in his chair, his legs up on his desk. He looked around when he heard Fury move.

'Felling any better?' he asked.

Fury got off his bunk and walked to the wall of the cell. He noticed his vomit was still on the floor.

'You letting me out?' he asked.

'I sure am,' the sheriff said. 'But I've ordered us food. It'll be here in an hour or so. It'll be close to nightfall then and

I figure on releasing you come first light.'

'I'd sooner go now,' Fury said.

'I let you out of there and you'll be straight after that other fella,' the sheriff said.

'I would,' Fury agreed.

The sheriff looked at Fury for several moments before answering.

'I'm sure you would,' he said and clamped another cigar between his teeth and brought a lucifer to it, striking it against his desk. 'And I don't doubt that someway down the road you'll do just that.'

'You got that right,' Fury said and realizing that it was no use arguing with the lawman he went back and sat upon his bunk. He wondered where the half-breed kid was, what he was doing. Had he left town when the sheriff had taken Fury in? Was he waiting around for Fury to be released? Not that it made any real difference. It was not as if the kid could bust him out — all he could do was sit tight and hope that the sheriff released him before he realised he was a wanted by the law.

With these thoughts running through his mind, Fury closed his eyes again.

8

Night had fallen but Sam Billings hadn't slowed his pace none and he continued to spur his horse forward each time the beast showed signs of faltering.

He wasn't sure if the sheriff had released Fury yet, but all the same he wasn't taking any chances and wouldn't stop until he found the herd, which he guessed by now would have reached the banks of the Sierra Blanca. If he kept up this pace he could reach them by sunup.

Billings figured that as soon as he had told his brother that Fury had been in Cash City they'd both quit the cattle drive and put some serious distance between themselves and Thomas Fury. Hide out somewhere that Fury would never find them and remain there until they got word that Fury was dead.

There were gunmen out looking for Fury and Billings had no doubt that sooner or later, one of them would get him.

'Come on,' he screamed and once again spurred his horse forward, cruelly digging the star-shaped rowel of his spur deep into the horse's flesh.

Eventually though, the horse did begin to slow and no matter how roughly Billings treated her she wouldn't give him any more speed. Billings knew that if he continued at this pace then pretty soon the horse would stop for good, exhausted, her heart no longer able to sustain the pace.

There was a stream ahead and although Billings couldn't see it in the darkness, he could hear it softly trickling over the stony ground.

He dismounted and led the horse towards the sound of the water.

'Come on, girl,' he said kindly, but with the scent of water in her nostrils the horse seemed to have found new legs and went eagerly towards the water. 'Sorry for riding you so. I just had to get away.' Billings patted the side of the horse's head as he spoke. He didn't consider himself to be cruel and treated his horse as well as the next man, but he was terrified of Fury catching up with him, and even now with miles between him and the town of Cash City he didn't feel any safer. He wouldn't feel safe until he had located the herd and spoken to his brother.

Perhaps not even then.

Deke would know just what to do, Billings told himself. His brother always seemed to know what to do.

Billings knelt besides the stream while the horse lapped at the cool water. He heard movement behind him, cleared leather and turned but there was nothing to be seen. He remained perfectly still for several moments, straining his ears and then decided that his imagination was getting the better of him. He was so worried about Fury that he was jumping at shadows.

And who could blame him for his nerves.

They'd already killed Fury once but it seemed they hadn't killed him good enough. He'd certainly seemed dead, lying there on the ground unmoving while they did what they'd done to his wife, and yet somehow Fury had survived, recovered even and then months later turned up spitting vengeance from his guns. He was getting closer and leaving a pile of bodies in his wake. He'd killed Cole Thornton, Ethan Tanner and Ethan's pa.

Back in Cash City, Fury had come mighty close to adding Billings to that list.

If it weren't for that sheriff, then Sam had no doubt he would now be just another name on Fury's list of kills.

There was a reddening on the far horizon, dawn still being a couple of hours away and Billings figured to rest the horse for a hour and then move out just before first light. He sat back on the ground and pulled his makings from his shirt pocket. He quickly put together a smoke and struck a lucifer on a boot heel. He sucked the smoke deep into his lungs, feeling it calm his nerves. After the hard ride it tasted good, perhaps the best tasting smoke he'd ever had.

Billings sat there and eventually he started to doze. He wasn't sure how long he'd slept before the sound of movement brought him awake in a panic. He cleared leather but realised that the sound had come from his horse, which had taken its fill of the water and was now grazing on the long grasses at the water's edge.

'Damn, I'm jumping at my own shadow.' Billings stood up and put together another quirly and then mounted his horse. He spurred the horse forward, though this time moving at a steady rather than breakneck pace. The dawn was fast approaching and Billings was starting to feel easier, though every now and then he looked over his shoulder, half expecting to see Fury on the distant horizon, but he saw nothing.

9

'The kid rode out,' the old man said as he handed Fury the reins of his horse. 'He paid everything up, though. You don't owe me a single cent.'

Fury looked at the old man, recognising him as the man who had run for the sheriff when he'd had Billings cold in his sights. He didn't hold it against the old man though, since he'd had no idea what had been going on, what this was all about. All he had seen had been two men shooting up his stables.

'Obliged,' Fury said and led the horse out of the stable and onto the street where the sheriff sat his horse, waited for him.

Fury climbed into his saddle and turned to face the lawman. 'I ain't coming back to this town,' he said. 'I'm riding straight on out of here. You can just as well give me my guns here and now and save yourself a ride.'

'Just the same I'll ride along with you to the town border,' the lawman said. 'It's such a lovely day for a ride and besides I'm sure a talkative fellow, you will appreciate the company.'

Despite himself, Fury gave a tight smile at that. He kicked his horse forward and the lawman took up the same pace, riding besides him.

As they rode, Fury wondered how far away the kid was. He didn't blame him for riding out on him. After all, the kid said he had killed a man, had even thought the two bounty hunters up in the mountains had been trailing him. Likely the law had spooked him, couldn't blame him for that. Of course he'd also run off when the bounty hunters had shown up, but that time he'd returned and pretty much saved Fury's life. Fury wondered if the kid was laying in wait even now, that any moment a well-aimed stone would unhorse the sheriff.

He sure hoped not. All he wanted to do now was to leave the sheriff behind and ride out after Billings. He been lucky so far in that the sheriff hadn't seen any wanted posters on him, and the sooner they reached the town border and he was left alone the better he would feel.

As it turned out they reached the town border without incident and the lawman handed Fury's guns over, together with the money Fury'd had in his pocket when he'd been arrested.

Fury hitched his gun belt, reached across and took his rifle from the sheriff. He slid it into his boot.

'I guess this is where we part company,' the lawman said.

Fury nodded, said nothing and spurred his horse into a gallop.

The lawman sat his horse for several long moments, watching until Fury became little more than a speck on the distant horizon, then turned and, keeping a steady pace, started back to town.

Tracking Billings was not an option, he'd had too much of a head start for that. The ground Fury now travelled upon was sun baked to such an extent that a herd of stampeding buffalo would be hard pushed to leave a mark. This meant that the only option would be to ride on to Tombstone and hope to catch up with Billings there. Fury knew that the chance he'd had back in Cash City to kill Billings would mean that Sam had likely ridden out after his brother with the news that he was after them. News that would put the Billings brothers on guard, send them into hiding.

Fury had travelled maybe five miles when he spotted a scrawny-looking desert rabbit foraging in a sorry-looking clump of greenery up ahead. The rabbit didn't seen to be aware of the approaching rider, likely the desert breeze had masked any sound or then again the rabbit's hunger could have gotten the better of it. Either way, the rabbit's carelessness meant that Fury had the chance of a decent meal.

Fury brought his horse to a stop with a gentle tap of spurs into the creature's side, and slid his rifle from the pouch he wore slung over his back.

He took careful aim and squeezed the trigger.

There was a loud retort and the rabbit spun around, seemed to run a few feet and then lay still on the desert ground.

'Got ya,' Fury whispered and slid the rifle back into the pouch.

Fury climbed from his horse and ran over to retrieve his kill. He'd not had a chance to collect the supplies he'd needed back in town, what with Billings popping up as he had in the general store, and his saddlebags contained nothing but a few handfuls of beans and a little jerky. This made the rabbit, no matter how scrawny, most welcome. Fury's stomach did a quick dance at the prospect of the meal. After so much dried jerky, the thought of fresh meat was especially welcome.

It was close to noon, the sun high in the sky and Fury decided that now would be a good time to rest up. He had kept a steady pace since leaving Cash City but all the same he couldn't risk tiring his horse. It was hot enough now but soon the sun would be punishing and so Fury ground-tied his horse, sat himself down on a large rock and set about skinning the rabbit.

He'd prepare the scrawny little critter, put together a small fire and, scraggy desert rabbit or not, sit down to likely the best meal he'd eaten in what seemed an age.

10

There were men everywhere and they weren't trying to hide. As they rode into the valley Tabor noticed men scattered in small groups, positioned around the valley walls. Wooden barricades had been constructed at several points and Tabor could see shooters positioned behind them. There were other men on the road ahead of them and all watched as Tabor and the sheriff rode towards the ranch house.

'Ain't no way Fury's gonna get in here,' the sheriff said. 'Not with all these men just waiting for him to put in an appearance.'

Tabor looked at the sheriff.

'Then why does Marlow need me?' he asked.

'Your job,' the sheriff said, 'is to stop Fury before he even gets here.

Mr Marlow don't take anything for granted.'

'I can see that,' Tabor said, though he wondered just how effective any of these men would be in the heat of battle.

They reached the ranch house, getting curious looks from all of the men as they rode past. Of course, the men weren't interested in the sheriff, but in Tabor, the gunman known across the country for being the most brutal, the most deadly of all the bounty killers.

Marlow came out to meet them but as he stepped down from the boardwalk and onto the sun-baked ground, he turned back to the house and saw his daughter framed in the doorway.

'Go back inside,' he said and when she didn't immediately comply but continued to stare at the two men riding towards them, he added, 'Listen to your father.'

Ellie frowned but turned on her feet and went back into the house.

'Yes Sir,' she said with a sarcastic military salute.

'This here's Haw Tabor,' the sheriff said as he dismounted. He groaned at the ache in the small of his back and looked at Marlow. The sheriff gave a shrug of his shoulders, as if to say he had no option but to bring the gunman here.

'Mr Tabor,' Marlow said and stepped forward, holding out a hand.

Tabor simply stood there, looked at Marlow's outstretched hand but made no move to take it.

Marlow frowned slightly, said, 'I've heard a lot about you. Your reputation speaks of excellence in your chosen line of business.' He didn't like the fact that the sheriff had brought the man here, but he guessed he would have had no choice in the matter. Mr Tabor seemed like a man who wouldn't take no for an answer and Hoskins was hardly the most forceful of men.

'I kill people,' Tabor said, thoughtfully. For a moment he seemed to be chewing on the words but then he smiled, said, 'Guess you could call it a line of business.'

'Indeed you could,' Marlow said, determined not to let his unease show. There was a coldness to Haw Tabor, which Marlow felt keenly. He had met some bad men in his time, but this was the first time he had stood before someone who was truly evil. Even the worst of men would have redeeming qualities but not this man, and Marlow had the feeling that it wasn't the financial reward that drove the man to kill, but rather the enjoyment of the kill itself.

'Mr Tabor's the best in the business,' the sheriff said, filling a chunk of silence that might have been three miles wide.

'I know my job,' Tabor said and removed his pipe from his pocket. He leisurely filled the bowl with tobacco and continued, 'I just like to meet the man who hires me. Face to face, eye to eye. Just to make sure there are no misunderstandings.' He brought a flame to his pipe and added, 'I don't like misunderstandings.'

'Refreshments,' Marlow said, again feeling ill at ease around the gunman. 'Come inside and we'll talk over business with something to drink.'

Tabor said nothing but followed the sheriff and Marlow into the house.

Marlow took them directly through to his office, where he offered whiskey. The sheriff took a glass but Tabor declined, saying that a coffee would be preferable, strong and black would be just the thing. He'd already had the one shot of whiskey back in town and wanted to keep a clear head.

Ellie brought in the coffee and was quickly ordered back out of the room by her father. She frowned and hesitated in the doorway, before leaving. She slammed the door harder that was necessary but declined to make any military gestures, sarcastic or otherwise.

Marlow shook his head, and lit one of his cigars. He held out the box to the other two men. The sheriff accepted but

Tabor simply shook his head and brought another match, which he struck on his boot heel, to his pipe. He never took his gaze from Marlow.

'Now how can I help you, Mr Tabor?' Marlow asked, speaking through a pungent cloud of rich tobacco smoke.

'What I want to know,' Tabor said after sipping at his coffee, 'is why is Fury so hell bent on coming after you?'

Marlow glared at the gunman. He was furious, wasn't used to being questioned by those in his employ, but Tabor made him feel uneasy and he took a deep breath before answering.

'I'm paying you,' Marlow said. 'Does it matter what my beef with Fury is? Does it make any real difference to you? If you don't want the job . . . '

'I've taken the job,' Tabor said. 'The money is all that really concerns me, but the facts often help.'

'Bring me Fury,' Marlow said, 'and you'll get your money but I'd rather not go into detail. Suffice to say Fury has his reason, no matter how misguided he is in his hatred of my family.'

Tabor nodded, smiled. It was a cold smile without humour and totally failed to reach his eyes.

'It's your son he wants,' he said.

Marlow looked at Tabor for several moments before simply nodding and taking a large draw from his cigar. He turned to the sheriff, asked him to leave. The lawman's face said that he didn't like that, but all the same he nodded and left the room.

Marlow stood and started pacing, puffing away on his cigar so that plumes of smoke were left in his wake.

'My son,' he said. 'He's always been headstrong, ever since he was a child. I blame my late wife, his mother, God rest her soul, for this. She tended to indulge him a little too much. Women and their sons.'

Marlow paused but Tabor said nothing, continued to puff on his pipe.

'He — that's my son,' Marlow continued, 'and some other men, two of whom are dead, killed by Fury . . . Well,

my son and these men, they . . . '
Marlow's words trailed off into silence
as he searched for the words. What
could he say? His son had done a
terrible thing, he knew that but he
wouldn't accept that it was his son's
fault. The other men had led him
astray.

'Your son,' Tabor said, removing the
pipe from his mouth, 'and these other
men shot Fury and thinking him dead,
they violated and then killed his wife.
His pregnant wife.'

There was an uncomfortable silence
between the two men and then Tabor
added, 'Least that's the way I heard it.'

Marlow nodded, buried his face in
his hands.

'Ain't no wonder Fury's all bent on
killing these men,' Tabor pointed out,
his eyes trained intently on Marlow.

Marlow looked at Tabor then but the
gunman's face was expressionless and
revealed nothing of how he was feeling.
He shook his head, said nothing.

'Some might say your son deserves

killing,' Tabor said. 'Did you know Fury's wife was with child?'

'You seem to know an awful lot,' Marlow snapped back, unable to hold his anger further. Who did this man, a hired gun when all was said and done, think he was to question him like this?

'Before I take any job,' Tabor said, 'I like to get the full facts. Weren't hard to discover what's behind Fury's rampage. Folks are talking about it across the territory but I don't like to listen to tittle-tattle and prefer to get the details first hand. From the look on your face, though, I get the feeling that the tittle-tattle may have been right on the button.'

With any other man the words would have sent Marlow into a fury, but there was darkness in his gunman's eyes that made Marlow hold his tongue. He made fists, digging his nails into his palms.

'Do you have children?' Marlow asked after a short silence.

Tabor smiled and shook his head.

'I ain't really the family kind,' he said. 'In my line of business raising a family could prove mighty tricky.'

'Then you could never understand,' Marlow said. 'What my son may or may not have done is irrelevant. I will not let him be gunned down like a dog.'

Once again a silence fell between the two men and Marlow sat there, shoulders slumped forward. He seemed to have aged ten years in as many minutes and his brash manner had vanished, leaving him feeling as timid as a newborn kitten. It wasn't a feeling he was used to.

'My son's paid for what he did,' Marlow said, as though trying to convince himself of the fact. 'I won't let Fury gun him down.'

'Where is he?' Tabor asked.

'Why do you need to know?'

'I've seen your daughter,' Tabor said. 'But I don't see no boy around here.'

'He's here,' Marlow said. 'And he's paid all he's going to for his part in what happened.'

'He's here? In this house?'

Marlow nodded. 'He's here.'

'Well if your son is here,' Tabor said, 'that just leaves the two Billings boys. Any idea where they are?'

'Last I heard they'd signed on as cowhands at a ranch just outside Tombstone. In the light of everything that happened I didn't want them working for me.'

'Which ranch?'

'The Circle Z.'

Tabor smiled, coldly. 'Well, maybe Fury figures they'll pay for their part in all this next. Before collecting on your son, that is.'

'My son's paid for his part in all this,' Marlow repeated. There was an audible crackle in his voice as if he were close to tears.

'Some would say there's only one way to pay for what these men done,' Tabor said, sending out plumes of smoke as he spoke. 'And that's with death. Fury's got a hatred for your son, a hatred that is understandable.'

Marlow stood up, unable to hold his anger.

'I don't pay you to lecture me,' he said. 'I pay you to bring me Fury. If it bothers you what my son did then turn around and ride out of here. I know what my son did and he's paid for it. Believe me he's paid for it, death ain't the only way to pay the piper.'

'No matter,' Tabor said, unsure of what Marlow meant but not really caring. He stood up. 'Have my money ready.'

Marlow nodded and watched as the gunman turned on his feet and left the room.

11

Rake had spotted Billings two days after leaving town.

The kid had been setting traps, hoping to snare a jackrabbit, when he'd noticed the man, heading east, riding his horse like he had the devil on his tail, but there had been no sign of Fury which puzzled the kid. Why was Billings pushing his horse like that when there didn't appear to be anyone in pursuit? Billings hadn't noticed the kid and Rake decided to keep it that way. For some time he had remained hidden while he watched Billings race through the valley below him.

The kid had then decided to follow the man and did for several miles, keeping a safe distance so as not to be seen, even following him through the night. All the while Rake wondered what it was that had provoked Fury into attacking him back in town. Fury had been all set to kill the man and likely would have, had not the town sheriff intervened.

Now though, Billings had met up with several other men who had been watering a herd of fine-looking horses in the river below. And the kid decided he would be best getting away from here. If he were spotted, he wouldn't only have to face Billings but the other men too. This wasn't his argument and indeed he had no clear idea what the beef between Fury had Billings was about.

The kid had turned his horse and rode back in the direction he had come, figuring he would put some distance between himself and the men and decide where to go from there.

Maybe he should try and find Fury. After all, it stood to reason that if the man called Billings had been released from the jailhouse then surely Fury had also been set free. Mind you, it was Fury who had attacked Billings so the kid guessed there was no guarantee that Fury wasn't still rotting in the jailhouse.

* * *

Deke sucked the last life out of the quirly and flicked it onto the ground. He allowed the smoke to hiss out between his teeth and shook his head as he looked at his brother.

'Damn that Fury,' he said. His brother Sam had ridden into camp not more than ten minutes ago. He had been breathless, terrified and had quickly taken Deke aside and told him of coming across Fury in Cash City, of being attacked by the man and if not for the actions of the town sheriff, he had no doubt that he would be dead.

'We knew he'd come for us,' Sam said, as he finished telling the story to his brother.

'Yeah,' Deke spat. 'I just figured one of them bounty killers would get him before he got anywhere near us.'

'That don't seem to be so.' Sam

pointed out the obvious.

'No, I can see that,' Deke took the makings from his shirt and quickly put together another quirly. He placed it between his chipped teeth and brought a match to it, sending a wisp of thin smoke onto the afternoon air.

'So what do we do now?' Sam asked presently.

'You figure Fury's going to come after us?' Deke spoke through a cloud of cigarette smoke.

Sam nodded.

'The sheriff back at Cash City was going to give me a head start and then set Fury free. The lawman didn't want us having our fight in his town, said he didn't care what we did to each other after that.'

Deke shook his head, ran a hand through the week's worth of stubble on his chin.

'Then I guess we'd better ride out,' he said, looking back at the other men who were gathered around the camp-fire. 'Sure do hate to ride out on this outfit, though. I kinda liked working this outfit.'

Sam looked at his brother, shrugged his shoulders as if to say that they had no choice. Sooner or later Fury would catch up with them and remaining with the outfit wasn't really an option. They needed to get as far away as possible, as quickly as possible.

12

Fury slid his field glasses from his saddlebags, muttered soothingly to steady his horse and lifted the glasses to his eyes. A thin smile crossed his lips as he focused the lens and brought the figure in the valley below into clarity.

So that's what had happened to the kid.

The kid was lying on the ground, peering into the slow-running river. He had both hands in the water, obviously trying to tickle a fish into his grasp.

Fury again steadied his horse, which was getting skittish. They had ridden for more than ten miles through nothing but featureless desert and had now reached an area of lush greenery and rolling grasslands. The river in the valley below looked cool and clear and after the long ride, the scent of the water was threatening to drive the horse into frenzy. The horse tried to move forward, eager to reach the water and Fury had to give several sharp tugs on the reins to bring it under control.

Fury watched the kid for several moments before slowly setting his horse off down the hill and into the valley. The ground beneath them was unsteady and Fury had to be careful as he guided the horse around one hazard after another.

'Hello below,' he shouted as he reached the halfway point and the kid immediately jumped up and then dropped down onto one knee and pulled his gun. He hadn't improved none with the weapon and Fury could have shot him three times over in the time it took him to clear leather.

'That ain't no kind of welcome,' Fury joshed.

'Fury,' the kid said and stood back up, holstering his gun. 'You plumb near scared the life out of me.'

'Kind of jumpy, aren't you?' Fury retorted.

The kid shrugged his shoulders and slid his gun back into its holster. It looked incredibly big in his small hand.

Fury soothed his horse as they reached the valley floor and spurred it over to the river's edge, where the kid was standing watching Fury approach.

'Well,' Fury said as he dismounted and allowed his horse to go to the river. 'Guess we meet again.'

The kid shrugged his shoulders.

'Guess we do,' he said.

Fury took his makings from his pocket and quickly put together a quirly. He struck a lucifer on the heel of his left boot and sucked the smoke to life.

'Wondered what became of you,' he said.

The kid shrugged his shoulders.

'When I saw the sheriff take you away to the jailhouse,' the kid said, 'I figured it was safer for me to ride out of town.'

'With you being a wanted man and all,' Fury said, smiling. 'I guess that was wise.'

The kid looked at Fury, unsure if he was being mocked. He pointed to the three fish on the ground.

'This time I can share my food with you.'

Fury looked at the fish. They were all rainbow trout and a decent size to boot. Cooked gently, they would make a delicious meal.

'That sounds good,' he said. 'I'm getting mighty tired of jerky and grits.' He didn't think the desert rabbit he'd eaten earlier was worth mentioning.

'I'll catch another one,' the kid said. 'They're plentiful. That's if your horse don't go scaring them all off.'

Fury laughed and looked at his horse. The beast had buried its muzzle in the river and was greedily slurping the cool water. Fury went and coaxed the horse away from the river, he didn't want it upsetting its stomach, and ground-tied it next to the kid's horse, which was happily grazing on the long grass of the valley floor.

'I'll set us a fire,' Fury said, feeling

his stomach rumbling at the prospect of fresh fish.

By the time Fury managed to get a fire going, the kid had coaxed a further two fish out from beneath the river bank, one of them a particularly large rainbow trout and with the aid of a pocket knife he skilfully prepared the fish for cooking, by roasting over a spit Fury had snapped off a nearby hackberry tree. They would eat well tonight.

The fish made a delicious meal and after they had eaten, Fury sat there smoking while they both gazed into the flames of the fire as the night slowly took over the skies above them.

'Why were you chasing that fella back in Cash City?' the kid asked presently.

Fury looked at the kid and his features clouded over. He flicked the remains of his quirly into the fire and shook his head.

'Because I'm going to kill him,' Fury said simply.

The kid looked at Fury and for a

moment he seemed to be considering pushing Fury for a reason, but then he thought better of it. He spat into the fire and said, 'I guess you got your reasons.'

'I sure do,' Fury said.

'Well you ain't going to catch him now,' the kid said. 'He's joined up with some cattle outfit a few miles down river.'

Fury looked at the kid and the look on his face seemed to darken as the fading light cast shadows that accentuated his cheekbones and turned his lips blood-red.

'I guess you'd better tell me what you know,' he said.

The kid told Fury of how he had come across Billings and followed him a' ways, trailing him until he'd met up with those men herding the cattle a few miles down river. The kid said that there had been at least twelve men among the cattle drive, likely a few more. He hadn't hung around to count heads and had ridden away as soon as

Billings had joined up with the other men. Didn't want to get spotted, the kid had pointed out, and have to explain to the men why he had been tracking Billings.

Fury didn't say a word and got to his feet, went to his horse.

'Where you going now?' the kid asked.

Fury turned back to face the kid. 'I'm going after those men,' he said and then climbed into the saddle.

'I told you,' the kid said, 'there's a whole bunch of men with Billings. You can't face them all.'

'No,' Fury nodded. 'That's about right but it's only Billings I'm interested in and his brother. Likely his brother's with him.'

The kid could see there was no use arguing with Fury and he shrugged his shoulders and made his way to his own horse.

'I guess I'll tag along,' he said.

'As you want,' Fury said. 'It's a free country and you can pretty much go anywhere you chose.'

'Sure,' the kid said and spurred his horse off after Fury, who had already taken the lead and was not going to wait for him. Looked like they would be riding through the night.

13

Fury looked at the trail boss and ran a hand through the stubble on his chin.

'You want to tell me what business it is of yours?' the man asked. He was dressed in a faded shirt, leather waistcoat and canvas pants and didn't look to be wearing a gun. The men behind him, Fury counted eight of them, were all wearing six shooters.

'Not really,' Fury said. 'I'm just looking for them. Those Billings boys owe me.'

'I figured they was running from something,' the man said, and turned his back on Fury while he went to the campfire and took a tobacco pouch from a bedroll on the ground. He put together a smoke and then turned back to Fury, sucking the quirly to life as he spoke. 'Sam rode back into camp like he had the devil on his tail and then him and his brother skedaddled out of here, left me short of men. I've got to get these here cattle back to Tombstone and I need every hand I can get. Whatever this is about between you and the Billings, it's a damn inconvenience for me.'

'Sorry about that,' Fury said, shifting in his saddle. 'I truly am.'

Dawn had been breaking by the time Fury and the kid had caught up with the cattle drive. The kid had expected them to hang back, weigh up the situation but Fury had simply rode directly into the camp. The cowboys had been eating breakfast in preparation, got the long day ahead of them and they all watched as Fury rode in with the kid tailing behind him. He'd nodded his head to one man after another, tipping his hat all polite, not wanting to appear a threat to the cowboys with whom he had no beef at all. He seemed perfectly relaxed, as though out for a leisurely ride, but the kid was aware that Fury's muscles were coiled, ready to spring into action at the first sign of trouble.

The man they were now speaking to had identified himself as the trail boss and he had approached Fury and the kid with caution, but he was aware that his men were behind him and would back him if things turned nasty. Fury had simply nodded in greeting and asked about the Billings boys.

'Which way did they go?' Fury asked the trail boss. The man simply looked at him, unsure if he should volunteer further information to the unshaved man with the cruel-looking eyes. He drew hard on his quirly, blowing a cloud of blue grey smoke into the air.

'You know, mister,' the trail boss said. 'I can offer you boys coffee, maybe a little something to eat. There's beans left in the pot and they'll only go to the critters when we ride out. My boys have eaten their fill.'

'Obliged but let the critters eat,' Fury said, which annoyed the kid. They had ridden through the night and the taste of the fish supper they'd eaten was now a distant memory, but he said nothing and simply sat his horse, watching the exchange between Fury and the trail boss.

'As you wish,' the trail boss said and turned to his men for a moment, shouting out orders, telling them to prepare to ride out, before turning back to Fury and adding, 'Makes no odds to me what you and the Billings boys got between you. They rode out east.'

'They didn't say where they were heading?'

'No,' the trail boss said, shaking his head. 'They rode off at a fair lick. Didn't say a word. Just went.'

'Obliged,' Fury said, tipped his hat in thanks and spurred his horse off, leaving the kid to catch up.

★   ★   ★

They had ridden for several miles without a word being said between them, not really pushing their horses but all the same keeping a steady pace, when Fury suddenly froze and pulled on the reins. Stopping his horse dead he raised a hand, indicating the kid do likewise.

'What is it?' the kid asked.

'Quiet,' Fury said and carefully slid from the saddle. He filled one of his hands with a Colt, took his field glasses from his saddlebags and motioned for the kid to hold back, remain where he was, while he cautiously walked towards the point where the trail crested the hill and started its long descent down the other side.

The kid sat his horse and watched Fury cautiously climb the hill. There was no indication of what had spooked Fury and Rake was puzzled. It was as if Fury had sensed some danger and yet everything seemed fine to the kid. He was the one with the Indian blood and he hadn't heard or seen anything. It was a fine afternoon and other than the sound of distant hawks there seemed to be total silence.

Fury had by now reached the crest of the hill and he stood there, his field glasses held to his eyes. He remained there for a few moments and then returned to the kid and climbed back into the saddle. He holstered the Colt and looked at the kid.

'There's a small wagon set besides the river a mile or so ahead,' Fury informed Rake and took the makings from his pocket and put together a quirly.

'A wagon.' Rake looked across at Fury. 'How many people?'

Fury shrugged his shoulders.

'Couldn't see anybody,' he said. 'Only the wagon.'

'How did you know?' the kid asked. 'I didn't hear anything.'

Fury looked at the kid and grinned before setting his horse off again.

'I can smell their campfire,' he said.

The kid sniffed the air. There was nothing he could detect and when he looked to the far horizon he could see no signs of smoke in the clear afternoon air. He shook his head, thinking this Fury was more of an Indian than he was.

As they neared the wagon the kid noticed Fury starting to tense, as if expecting trouble. Suddenly there was movement from the wagon as a man jumped out of the door flaps and yawned. The man hadn't noticed the approaching riders and he adjusted his pants, removed his pecker and proceeded to relieve himself against one of the wagon wheels. The man pulled a bottle of whiskey from his pocket and took a gulp as he continued to send a steady stream of urine onto the wheel.

Fury cast a glance at the kid, his eyes seeming to implore caution.

'Hello there,' Fury yelled as they came ever closer to the wagon.

The man turned, surprised but continued urinating for a moment. Then he took another sip of his whiskey, placed his pecker back in his pants and adjusted his clothing. The whiskey bottle was now empty and the man tossed it to the ground and wiped his hands on the back of his pants.

'Howdy,' he said.

Fury noticed the man wasn't armed but another man, who jumped from the wagon, most certainly was. The man was holding a gleaming Winchester rifle and pointing it directly in Fury's direction.

Again Fury gave the kid a quick glance and then turned his attention to the two men standing by the wagon.

'We're two travelling men passing through,' Fury said now that they were closer enough to the wagon for the men to hear them without the need to yell. 'Pleased to make your acquaintance.'

'Well, keep right on passing,' the man with the rifle said, earning himself a look of reproach from his companion.

'Now Tad,' the man, who only moments ago had been pissing against the wagon, said. 'That ain't very friendly. Where you folks heading?'

'Just drifting,' Fury replied and pulled his horse to a halt besides the wagon. For a moment he thought he heard movement from within the wagon and he waited for someone else to emerge, but no one did. He carefully appraised the two men; the man with the rifle was younger than the other but not by more than a few years. Both men were, Fury guessed, in their fifties and both had similar features, which suggested to Fury that they were brothers, or some kind of kin at least.

'You'll have to pardon my brother,' the first man said. 'He never was the sociable kind.'

Fury nodded, smiled wryly.

'So what can we do for you fellas?' the man asked and motioned for his brother to lower his rifle. Tad, though, ignored his brother and kept his rifle at the ready while his eyes darted from Fury to the kid and then back again.

'Like I said, we're just passing through,' Fury said. 'We're looking for two men, friends of ours. Don't suppose you two seen anyone these last few days?'

'Hell we — ' the first man said but he was cut off by his brother.

'Shut up, Clem,' Tad said. 'You always was one to run off at the mouth.'

The man called Clem frowned. 'We can't offer you men much in the way of hospitality,' he said. 'We barely got enough to feed ourselves but you're welcome to a pot of coffee. I was just going to get some boiling.'

'Well, you're welcome to a little coffee,' Tad said and then turned his attention to Rake. 'But you're Indian ain't.'

'Now Tad,' Clem said. 'There you go again. Once more I apologise for my brother's sour nature.'

Fury looked across at Rake and shrugged his shoulders.

'He ain't my Indian,' he said.

'I ain't no one's Indian,' Rake put in, indignantly.

'That's about the measure of it,' Fury said. 'Rake here's a free man. He pretty much comes and goes as he pleases.'

'I don't chow down with no Indian,'

Tad said and his finger tensed a little on the trigger of the rifle.

'Now that ain't strictly true, is it?' Clem said and laughed. The meaning of his remark was lost on both Fury and the kid but his brother offered a tight smile in response.

'We'll be riding on,' Fury said and then shifted in his saddle, adding, 'You ain't answered my question.'

'What question was that?' Tad asked.

'You seen two men riding about this way?' Fury was growing tired of the two men, and reckoned that if it came to a play he would be able to clear leather and put a slug between the man's eyes before he got to pull the trigger of that gleaming Winchester rifle.

'We ain't seen nobody,' the man with the rifle said.

'Obliged,' Fury said, tipped his hat and spurred his horse forward. He gave the kid another glance and its meaning was obvious. 'There's someone else in that wagon,' Fury said, speaking to the kid in little more than a whisper.

The kid nodded. He too had the same feeling.

'Keep going,' Fury said, again speaking in whispers. 'We'll come back when these two are not expecting it.'

'You think it could be the two men you're looking for?' the kid asked. 'Hiding in that wagon, I mean.'

Fury gave a non-committal shrug. He had of course considered the possibility but he didn't think it was likely that the two men were hiding in the back of the wagon. If the Billings brothers had been with those two men then likely they would have tried to gun down on Fury and the kid. From what Fury knew of men like the Billings, staging an ambush from concealment would be the sort of move that would appeal to them. If they had been in the back of that wagon then taking the chance to gun down Fury before he had the chance to react would be too good an opportunity for them to pass by.

'There was certainly someone in the back of that wagon,' Fury said.

151

'Someone those two didn't want us to see.' And that made him very curious and although he supposed it was none of his business, he was going to find out all the same.

Fury heard the sound of the hammer being pulled back on the rifle behind him and he spun in the saddle, clearing leather and shooting in one impossibly fluid movement. His aim was true and he hit the man with the rifle in the face, shattering teeth and bone as the man was thrown back onto the ground. The other man had now produced a pistol and he got off a shot but it went wide, Fury heard the slug whistling through the air. Again he fired, this time hitting the second man in the throat, killing him instantly.

Fury looked at the kid and shook his head.

'Damn fools had to make a play,' he said.

The kid was shocked by the sudden burst of violence. It had happened so quickly and had been over in a matter of seconds. All that remained was the sickly stench of cordite in the air. He watched as Fury turned his horse and made his way back to the wagon and then followed after him. In the time it had taken for Fury to turn and kill the two men, the kid hadn't even cleared leather.

Fury looked down at the two dead men. He knew nothing about them, the lives they had led but he sure knew a whole lot about the deaths they had died. He shook his head, thinking how pointless this all was and cursing the two men for forcing his hand. The kid too looked down at the two dead men, feeling his stomach churn as he saw the extent of their injuries. The man who had held the rifle was the worst and all that remained where his face had been was a glistening red mass of pulp. Already there were flies buzzing around the two dead men, drawn by the aroma of still-warm blood.

'Don't mind them,' Fury said and the kid wondered if he had eyes in the back of his head. 'They're critter food now.'

'Dumb bastards,' the kid said as Fury dismounted and went into the wagon, but any sympathy the kid felt for the two men soon vanished when he saw Fury emerge from the wagon, holding a terrified-looking Indian girl in his arms.

The girl was struggling and when her frightened eyes fell onto the two dead men she screamed and broke free of Fury's hold. She ran to the men and fell down onto her knees between them both. Once more she screamed but then the scream faded and was replaced by manic laughter.

'You killed them,' she said finally and turned to look at Fury, who simply nodded in reply.

14

It hadn't been difficult for Haw Tabor to find the Billings boys. Directly after leaving the Marlow ranch he'd taken the train, loading his newly purchased horse onto the livery carriage, and gone directly to Tombstone and the offices of the Circle Z cattle company which employed the brothers. He'd been told by an irate office worker that both of the Billings boys had until a few days ago been part of an outfit bringing a herd in across the flats but had deserted the outfit, just skedaddled leaving the outfit short-manned. The foreman had sent a rider into town to request a couple of replacement hands, and they were promptly on their way. The Billings boys hadn't given any reason for their departure so close to completing the job, which the office worker said made no sense — but Tabor could guess the reason behind the Billings' swift departure.

He guessed it meant Fury was closing in on them and that the brothers had become aware of this.

Tabor had thanked the office worker for his help and gone straight to the offices of the *Tombstone Epitaph* where he was shown maps of the territory. The newspaperman had been only too eager to talk to Tabor, and answered any questions to the best of his ability. It helped that Tabor carried a card that identified him as an agent of the Pinkerton Detective Agency and although the identification was false, Tabor had used it many times and not once had he been challenged. The Pinkerton name tended to open doors more often than a skeleton key. From the maps he was shown, and the knowledge of the area that the newspaperman gave, Tabor made a guess where he would find the Billings boys and he promptly rode due west of Tombstone until he came to the one-time mining town known as Carver's Crossing.

Carver's Crossing was just north of the Mexican border. The town had once prospered but unlike the large strikes of gold and silver in the nearby Cochise County, the loads found around Carver's Crossing had been much more modest and were worked out pretty darn quickly. Samuel Carver, a man who would blow his own head off with a shotgun after finding himself penniless once too often, had founded the town back in 1860, when he spent a long summer dodging Indians and prospecting for ore. His first strike produced some gold and a little silver and as word got out, other miners turned up and they were quickly followed by those who preyed on the nouveau riche; gamblers, prostitutes and gunmen. Before anyone could shake a possum's tail, a small town, named for the prospector and soon-to-be shotgun chewer, had sprung up. The mines had continued to pay out for a few years but the strikes became far less frequent and in 1877, a man named Ed Schieffelin struck a mother lode of silver only twenty-five miles away. That strike became known as the Tombstone Lode and pretty soon folks started abandoning Carver's Crossing for the more promising pickings further on up the trail. And so it was that the town of Tombstone grew while Carver's Crossing was left prey to the elements. These days the town provided shelter for drifters, outlaws and all manner of outcasts.

No one ever came to Carver's Crossing unless they were hiding and Tabor had rightly guessed that this was where the Billings brothers would chose to hide out until the problem with Fury had resolved itself. He'd left Tombstone, riding through the night, and reached Carver's Crossing shortly after dawn the next day. There was no law in the town, indeed the town no longer officially existed and only showed up on maps as being abandoned. The town had a small saloon, if you could call it that, and several buildings that were occupied by whichever low-life happened to be in the town at any particular time.

Tabor went straight to the saloon, which was always open, even at this early hour. There were several men at the various battered-looking tables; most of them were slumped forward, sleeping with their heads resting on their arms while half drunk glasses sat in front of them. There was a small, balding man with mean eyes standing behind the makeshift counter.

'Can I help you?' the barkeep asked, his eyes wandering over the heavily armed newcomer.

Tabor looked at the man, smiled.

'Little too early for me,' he said.

'Then what you come in here for?' The barkeep worried the side of his mouth with his tongue and then spat a lump of gristle, left over from his last meal, onto the counter.

Again Tabor smiled, said, 'For the

159

company I guess.'

The barkeep frowned, produced a half smoked cigar from behind one ear and placed it between his teeth.

Tabor removed his pipe from a pocket and thumbed thick-cut tobacco into the bowl. He struck a lucifer on the counter, brought it to the bowl and sucked the pipe to life. Next he reached into another pocket and produced a ten-dollar bill and placed it on the counter.

'Thought you said it was too early,' the barkeep said, smiling around the cigar. 'What can I get you?'

'Information,' Tabor said, speaking himself through a thick cloud of fragrant smoke.

The barkeep's eyes went to the bill and then back to Tabor.

'I got some sour mash whiskey,' he said. 'A lot of beer, all brewed on the premises but I don't have much in the way of information. Town like this we don't much trade in tittle-tattle.'

'You must see everyone who comes

into this sorry excuse for a town.' Tabor savoured a mouthful of smoke. 'Being barkeep and there being no other signs of entertainment in this town, you must know what goes on around here, who comes in around here.'

'I'm blind in both eyes and deaf in each ear,' the barkeep said. 'I see nothing. I hear nothing. It's the only way to stay healthy in a town like this.'

Tabor smiled and reached into his pocket and pulled out another bill, a twenty this time. He placed it on top of the ten.

'Eyesight improved any?' he asked.

'Depends.'

'On what?'

'On what you want to know.'

Tabor took a glance around him. None of the men seated at the tables appeared to be awake. He took his time, allowing his eyes to travel the full length of the saloon before turning back to the barkeep.

'I'm looking for two men,' he said. 'Would have rode in here over the last few days, certainly no longer than four days ago. Cowboys, both in their late twenties and likely carrying a lot of trail dust with them.'

The barkeep made to grab the money but Tabor's hand shot out and pinned the man's hand flat to the counter. He caught the barkeep in a stare and held it.

'You ain't earned that money yet,' Tabor snarled.

'Just so happens,' the barkeep said, 'I know of two men who fit that description. They came in two days ago and seem to be intent on staying awhile.'

Tabor released the man's hand, allowed him to scoop up the money, which he did and promptly stuffed it into his pocket.

'Where can I find these men?' Tabor asked.

'They're upstairs,' the barkeep said. 'Went up late with two of my girls and they ain't come down yet.'

'They're up there now?'

The barkeep nodded.

Tabor considered this information for a moment. If it were the Billings boys up there then he could see no reason to announce his presence. All he needed to do was ensure that it was the brothers, then keep a safe distance but make sure he remained close by because, he knew, Fury would turn up sooner or later. For all he cared Fury could blow the two Billings boys to hell, just as long as he took Fury down before he got to the Marlow place. That was what he was being paid for and nothing else really mattered.

'I tell you what I'm going to do,' Tabor said, leaning over the counter and speaking quietly to the barkeep. 'I'm gonna take me a seat over there and wait for them two men to come down. Do you do food in this hell hole?'

The barkeep smiled, said, 'Likely I could rustle something up.'

'You do that,' Tabor said and went and took a table with a good view of the rickety-looking stairs that led to the second floor.

For several moments the barkeep stood where he was, staring at Tabor and for a moment he considered going upstairs and warning the two men that he was here, but figuring it was none of his business, he shrugged his shoulders and went through to the back of the building to rustle up some bacon and beans.

15

Rake nodded and smiled at the girl.

'You are safe now,' he said and handed her a tin cup filled with coffee.

She was a full-blooded Apache, said her name was Bina, that she was the daughter of Tarak and Dehteste but her parents were dead, killed by the two men who now lay dead themselves, thanks to Fury's sharp shooting. She was pleased Fury had killed the men and had twice spat on their bodies.

The way the girl told it was that she and her parents, together with many of their people, had spent more than three summers on a white man's reservation. Her parents were elderly and they had gained the trust of the white men who guarded over them at the reservation. One morning, Tarak had simply gathered together his wife and daughter and ridden out of the reservation, claiming they had wanted to fish along the river as they were often allowed to do. The girl wasn't sure if her father had actually intended to fish for several hours and then return to the reservation as they had done many times before, but that was of no matter for the facts were that that day, Tarak had decided he was tired of the white man's ways and they didn't go back to the reservation as they usually did when the sun grew tired in the sky. Instead they rode out to the west, looking, the man had claimed, for land where they could live in peace, away from the false restraints of what the white men called 'civilisation'. Tarak said he had watched an eagle flying in the sky for some time and that the eagle had spoken to him, telling him to forsake the ways of the white man or the gods would be angry. And so it was that the old Indian, his wife and daughter had simply vanished into the wilderness.

No one thought to come looking for them, likely the white men figured the two aged Apaches and their daughter were not worth the trouble of a search party.

That, the girl said, had been a full summer ago and for some time they had lived in the mountains, existing on the fruits of the land but with winter approaching, Tarak knew that the land would not be able to provide for them and the eagle did not return to offer the old man further counsel. Reluctantly the old brave had decided to take his wife and daughter back to the reservation. They had been heading back that way when they came across the two men in the wagon, the men who called themselves Clem and Tad, the men who now lay dead on the ground before them, flies buzzing around, ready to claim their bodies.

At first Tarak had tried to trade with the men, showing them the beaver pelts he had tied to one of the horses, and the charms his wife had made from bones, stones and wood. The two white men had made a show of examining the

167

pelts, but it was clear that the only interest the two men had was in the young Indian girl. Bina had said that she didn't like the way the two men looked at her, especially Tad and when they had offered the old Indian man two bottles of whiskey for his daughter he had been offended, had cursed the two white men.

It had been then that the men had pulled their pistols and shot both the girl's mother and father. Bina had seen both her mother and father die, and at first she had expected to be shot down herself but the bullet had not come.

She was young and the men had other uses for her.

She had been with the men ever since.

'I think it would have been better had they shot me down,' the girl concluded and once again her eyes started to fill with tears.

Rake could imagine what the girl had gone through at the hands of the two men and he reached across and put a comforting hand on one of the girl's legs, noticing her flinch slightly.

'You are safe now,' he said again. 'No one is going to hurt you.'

The girl looked first at Rake and then at Fury. She smiled weakly and looked back at the two dead men, and when she turned back Rake noticed that the tears in her eyes had dried.

'Guess those two got what they deserved,' Fury said. 'But I'm looking for two different men. When I asked those two there about them they claimed they had not seen the men I seek, but I had the feeling they weren't telling me the truth.'

'There were two men,' Bina said. 'They passed us two days ago. Would these be the men you seek?'

'Describe them,' Fury said.

The girl did so and Fury nodded, seeing the image of the Billings brothers in his mind's eye as the girl spoke.

It was as if the girl's words painted a picture within Fury's mind.

It certainly looked like the Billings brothers.

Fury got up from his crouching position, went to the wagon and jumped back inside. A moment later he emerged, carrying a half sack of Folgers coffee and several packs of hard biscuits.

'Collect the food,' he said. 'Split it among our saddlebags.'

'Would it not be easier for us to take the wagon?' Rake asked.

'It'll only slow us down,' Fury said. 'I've got some men to find. It's pretty much up to you what you do.'

Rake watched as Fury once more climbed into the wagon and then he turned to Bina.

'You can travel with us,' he said. 'Take the best horse from the wagon team. I guess after all you've been through you kind'a have a right to a horse.'

The girl nodded, smiled and went and started scooping up the food that Fury had taken from the wagon. Next,

Fury emerged with several bottles of whiskey, two buffalo hides and a shotgun. The barrel of the shotgun had been sawn down considerably, making it a deadly weapon at close range.

'Ain't much more of use to us in there,' Fury said and dropped the items to the floor.

The Indian girl came to the shotgun, picked it up and broke the barrel. It was loaded. There was a strap made from rawhide fixed to the weapon and she slung it over her shoulder.

'I will keep this. I will need a weapon to defend myself from men such as these in the future.' She gestured with the shotgun at the two men.

Fury looked at the girl for a moment and then nodded.

'Guess you'd better look around for some shells for that thing,' he said. 'Ain't much use otherwise.'

'I know where they keep the ammunition for this,' Bina said and climbed into the wagon herself. She had often lain awake at night thinking of what it would be like to grab the shotgun and blow the two men's heads off while they slept.

'She is coming with us,' Rake said once Bina was inside the wagon and out of earshot.

'I guess so,' Fury said and took a quick glance back at the wagon. 'Looks like I'm building up quite an entourage.'

Rake nodded, smiled.

'We should just take the wagon,' he said.

Fury's face clouded over.

'No,' he said. 'The wagon will slow us down.'

He knew he would soon reach the end of the vengeance trail and that he would be better off alone when he did what had to be done. Rake and the girl could ride with him for a' ways but they would be better off going their own way further down the trail. It was not as if Rake was alone now; there were two of them, they were young and had their own lives to live, and they had no

business being involved in the deadly
business still ahead of Thomas Fury.

16

They had ridden for maybe ten miles, all of them hard with a merciless sun high in the sky and no breeze to move the air about when they came upon the carcass of the horse. Fury brought his horse to a halt, looked down at the dead animal. He cast a shadow over the remains and a posse of flies buzzed angrily for a moment and then went back to their meal.

Fury could see that one of the horse's legs was broken, the irregular angle of the limb told him that. The poor beast had likely stumbled, snapped the bone and then his rider had put it out of its misery with a slug to the side of the head. The gaping wound was visible, flies attached to the dried blood.

'The men you seek,' Bina said, as she and Rake caught up with Fury and sat their horses, 'one of them was riding this horse.'

Fury looked at the Indian girl, wiped a bead of sweat from his forehead.

'You sure?' he asked.

Bina nodded, said, 'The two riders I told you about. This horse belonged to one of them. I recognise the horse. It has the same markings. There is no doubt.'

The unfortunate horse, a paint, had no doubt been ridden too fast over too much of a distance and it was likely fatigue that had caused it to stumble and break the leg. If the two men Bina spoke of were the Billings boys then Fury guessed they had been in pretty much of a hurry to ride their horses in such a fashion. They would be riding two to a horse now, which would make them a damn sight easier to track. A horse carrying two men leaves different tracks to a horse carrying a single rider.

Fury guessed that the horse had been dead for no more than two days, which meant that he was fast closing in on the

Billings. Assuming of course that the two men were the Billings boys and Fury had every reason to believe that they were. Soon, he knew, he would have them in his gun sights and then all that would remain was Luke Marlow, and after that . . .

After that, what?

Fury didn't know. All that had occupied his mind for as long as he could remember now was getting vengeance for the killing of his wife and the child she had carried inside her. He had no idea what he would do after that, didn't really care and he couldn't really see any reason to go on once he'd done what had to be done.

Revenge was the only thing that drove him; it kept him alive, gave him a reason to go on.

He cast a glance over his shoulders at Rake and Bina who were riding abreast behind him. They seemed to be engaged in conversation, chatting away and this made Fury smile. It was good to see and he guessed that the best thing was if he separated from the two youngsters; they didn't need to be with him when he went looking for vengeance. They had both been through enough and had their own lives to lead, perhaps a life they would lead together. They were more or less of the same age and both were Indians, the girl full-blooded and Rake a half-breed.

Fury slowed his horse as they approached the shallow-looking river and for the first time he could see the tracks left by the Billings, or at least by the horse being ridden by two men.

He took his makings from the pouch he wore and quickly put together a quirly, struck a lucifer on his saddle and started off across the river, Rake and the girl following close behind.

★　★　★

Tabor wouldn't have approached the two Billings boys, had been content to sit back, keep his distance and wait until Fury turned up looking for them.

He'd spent the last two days in Carver's Crossing and in all that time he'd kept close to the two boys, hadn't announced himself but had shadowed them, which wasn't that difficult since they spent most of their time in the saloon, either drinking or whoring. Now though they seemed to be setting to leave town, and he didn't want that.

He didn't want that at all.

He watched them as they made a deal with a squat-looking Mexican for a couple of fresh horses, and it was then and only then that he crossed the dusty street and made himself known to them.

'Mister, you're crazy.' The speaker was Sam Billings and he was all ready to get on his horse and ride like hell. He certainly didn't want to wait around for Fury to get here. That option, as far as he was concerned, was akin to suicide. 'Fury damn near killed me back in Cash City. I was lucky then and I don't want to push my luck.'

'You ain't listening to me,' Tabor said

and when Sam made to answer back, his brother raised a hand to silence him. At least one of the Billings seemed to have a brain in his head.

'Go on,' Deke Billings said and made himself a quirly while he watched Tabor fill his pipe and lodge it between his teeth.

'I told you,' Tabor said. 'I'm working for Marlow and it's my job to kill Thomas Fury. Now, I know he's tracking you boys and I reckon he ain't too far behind. I don't want to go riding all over looking for him and would much rather he came to me and I figure with you boys here, he just might do that.'

'And then you'll kill him?' Sam Billings again.

'And then I'll kill him,' Tabor agreed, speaking through a cloud of thick smoke.

'What if he kills you first?'

Tabor looked at Sam Billings and smiled, said, 'That ain't likely.'

'Yeah well,' Sam Billings said. 'I

179

admire your grit, mister, but me and my brother would sooner ride out of here. Seems to me that's the best way to get away from Fury. That man ain't human. We killed him once and he's still coming after us.'

'Difference is,' Tabor said, 'when I kill someone they stay dead.'

'I don't know about this,' Deke Billings said and shook his head. He looked first at his brother and then turned back to Tabor. 'I've heard of you,' he said, 'and I know your reputation but all the same Thomas Fury is proving a hard man to kill.'

'You ride out, Fury comes after you,' Tabor said. 'And sooner or later he's going to catch up with you and then he's going to kill you. If you boys stay here we can end this here and now.'

'Yeah, end it with us dead,' Sam Billings said and again turned to his horse, but once more his brother stopped him.

Tabor smiled and watched as two men walked past. He watched them go down the street and into the saloon before turning back to the two brothers.

'That ain't going to happen,' he said. 'I'll get Fury before he gets to either of you two boys.'

'So what do you want us to do?' Deke asked.

'Not much,' Tabor said. 'You just go back to what you been doing.'

'We ain't been doing much of anything,' Sam said.

'You been drinking and whoring aplenty,' Tabor said. 'Do some more. Hell, I'll even stand you boys some money to do so.'

The Billings brothers looked at each other and then turned back to Tabor, smiling.

'I've been following reports of Fury,' Tabor said, 'and trying to figure out his movements. The fact that you saw him in Cash City pretty much proves I've been correct in figuring his route. Now I'm willing to wager he's going to show up here mighty soon. In fact, with you boys here I'm sure of it and when that happens I'm going to be close by. I'll take that son of a bitch down before he gets anywhere near either of you two.'

'You sure of that?' Sam asked.

'I'm sure,' Tabor said. 'I'm damn sure.'

'Then, mister,' Deke Billings smiled and held out his hand to Tabor, who took it and they shook, 'that's good enough for me.'

Sam Billings didn't offer his hand, but stood there looking troubled. He spat into the dirt and turned back to his brother.

'I hope you know what you're doing, Deke,' he said.

'Hell, I ain't too sure of anything,' Deke said. 'But I figure this man here knows enough for all of us.'

The Billings took their horses back to the fenced-off area that acted as a makeshift corral and then returned to meet Tabor outside the saloon.

'Glad to see you boys finally seeing some sense,' Tabor said and handed them twenty dollars apiece. 'A little enjoyment money,' he said.

And as the three men walked back into the saloon and out of the strong afternoon sunshine, Fury and his companions were less than twenty miles away, fast approaching Carver's Crossing.

17

Fury climbed from the saddle and ground-tied his horse.

He walked over to the ridge and looked down at Carver's Crossing. The town was on its last legs and if it weren't for the transient population — drifters, outlaws, army deserters — it would be a ghost town.

'Where is that?' Rake asked and stood beside Fury. Bina remained on her horse and watched the two men.

'That used to be somewhere.' Fury had passed through this way once during the war and knew of the town's history. He had heard tales of the times when Carver's Crossing had been in much better health. Back then it had been one of the great western towns, and yet where Tombstone, its neighbouring town, had prospered and continued to prosper, the town had been left to whither and decay like a carcass in the merciless afternoon sun.

'It don't look like much of a town to me,' Rake said. 'It even makes Cash City seem like one of those big towns back east that I keep hearing about.'

Fury smiled, said, 'That's about right.'

Bina dismounted and came to the edge of the ridge. She crouched down and stared at the town; a shadow seemed to fall across her features. She looked at Fury and the kid and both men saw the fear in her eyes.

'I don't want to go there,' she said.

'You don't have to go anywhere you don't want to,' Fury replied and took his makings and put together a smoke. 'You're free to ride out anywhere you want. You ain't answerable to anyone anymore.'

'I've been there,' Bina said. 'Those two men I was with. They took me there. It is an evil place, full of bad men.'

'It's bad men I'm looking for,' Fury

said. 'So I guess I'm riding in and I figure now is as good a time as any for us all to go our separate ways.'

Fury turned to look at Rake and Bina. He had a feeling about this and even if the Billings boys didn't turn out to be hiding in Carver's Crossing then he figured it wouldn't be long now before he caught up with them, and once that was done he'd move on to the Marlow place. He didn't need the boy and girl with him any longer, and whatever dangers he had to face, he'd much rather face them without his two companions.

They had no need to be a part of this.

'I'm with you,' Rake said and looked at Bina as if hoping she would say much the same thing, but the Indian didn't answer and merely nodded her head. She had only ridden with the two men a short time and figured she would much rather ride away, find her own people. She had the shotgun slung over her shoulder and would use it if the need arose, but only to defend herself from men like the two who had killed her parents and taken her by force. She certainly didn't want to ride into a gunfight, which was just what this man Fury seemed to be looking for.

'No,' Fury said and took his makings from the pouch he wore tied around his neck. He put together a quirly and looked at his two young companions for several moments before speaking. 'I need to go on alone. You two need to ride out together, find somewhere where you can make lives for yourselves.'

'What about you?' Rake asked.

'I started out on this alone,' Fury said. 'And it's only right I end it alone.'

Rake shook his head. He stood firm, staring at Fury.

'I don't even know what this is truly about,' he said. 'I've ridden with you for many miles now and I don't really know what this is about.'

'You know enough,' Fury said, went

back to his horse and climbed into the saddle.

'I'm coming with you,' Rake insisted.

'No.' Fury turned the horse and again looked at his companions. 'Look after the girl.'

Rake nodded.

'It's been good knowing you,' Fury said and spurred his horse towards Carver's Crossing, leaving Bina and Rake to watch his dust as he started the horse into a gallop.

★ ★ ★

Tabor saw Fury come into town; there was no mistaking the man from the wanted posters he'd seen and the descriptions he'd been given, but all the same he took the crumpled wanted poster from the breast pocket of his frock coat and smiled when he saw the image.

The man who had just ridden into town was Thomas Fury.

There was no doubt of that.

Tabor immediately backed himself into an alleyway between two derelict buildings and thumbed back the hammer of the Colt Paterson, but didn't pull it from the holster. The Billings boys were in the saloon and Tabor decided to watch how this played out before making his move.

Fury stopped his horse in the middle of the dusty street and looked around. Tabor watched him as he first looked up and down the street and he continued to watch Fury as he slowly led his horse towards the saloon.

'Come on, Fury,' Tabor whispered, a thumb smoothing the handle of the Colt Paterson. 'Go inside.'

Tabor remained where he was, watching as Fury climbed out of the saddle, tied his horse to a hitching rail and went into the saloon. Then and only then did Tabor pull the big old Colt Paterson and emerge from the alleyway.

He quickly made his way towards the saloon.

* * *

It took a moment for Fury's eyes to adjust to the gloom of the saloon interior but as soon as he could see, he noticed the Billings boys sitting at a table beside the bar. They were playing cards with another two men Fury didn't recognise and so far, neither of the Billings brothers had noticed Fury.

'Samuel and Deke Billings,' Fury yelled and slid the rifle out of the pouch slung over his shoulder. 'I'm going to kill you both.'

He saw Deke draw first and Fury took him out with a well-placed shot to the centre of his chest. The man was thrown over the table with the force and then chaos broke out. The two other men who had been playing cards with the Billings went for their own weapons but Fury was quicker, working the lever of the rifle he first shot one, and then the other. One of the men, Fury was not sure which, had managed to get off a shot and Fury heard it slam into the wall behind him.

'Don't shoot,' Sam Billings dropped his own weapon, a Remington, and held his arms up towards the ceiling. 'I ain't armed.'

'Neither was my wife,' Fury said coldly and shot Sam Billings square between the eyes, sending a spray of blood and brain matter splattering onto the floor where it was quickly soaked up by the dust.

Fury looked around the saloon but all he saw were shocked faces staring back at him; nobody pulled a gun. Fury slid his rifle back into its pouch and made to turn when he heard someone call his name from behind.

Fury cleared leather, filling a hand with one of his Colts and turning on his feet but it was too late and he heard the roar of the large calibre Colt Paterson before feeling the thunderous pain in his left side. He was thrown backwards, came down hard on the floor and looked up into the grinning face of a man with a brutal-looking scar that ran down the left side of his face and parted his lips.

'It's the end of the road for you, Fury,' Tabor said and laughed.

Fury looked up at the hideous gunman, the improbably large Colt Paterson held tightly in his hand.

'Who are you?' Fury managed and gritted his teeth against the red-hot pain that was spreading up from his stomach. He felt the sticky blood that was saturating his shirt and spreading out into a puddle on the floor.

'Haw Tabor. That name mean anything to you?'

'I heard of you,' Fury said, feeling warm blood on his lips as he spoke. 'Heard you're a cold-hearted son of a bitch.'

'That's about right,' Tabor said and laughed. He was about to put another shot into Fury when a shotgun sounded from behind him and the back of his head exploded in a gory spray of blood and scalp.

He didn't know what hit him and he

fell forward onto Fury, dead before he hit the floor.

Fury knew he had been hit good, perhaps fatally and the last thing he saw before blackness overtook him was Rake and Bina standing in the doorway of the saloon.

The Indian girl held a still-smoking shotgun in her hands.

18

Fury's wife was here; she held out a hand, beckoning her husband to her side.

'Rose,' Fury said. 'Rose. Is it you, Rose?'

'My husband,' Rose said and laughed. 'Who else would it be?'

Fury reached out for his wife's hand but then he felt a tremendous wave of pain and the image of Rose faded, drifted away into nothingness until all that remained was blackness.

An icy blackness.

Fury heard himself scream out but he didn't think the scream had emerged from his lips, and he fought against the pull of the blackness, wanted to see his wife again.

'Thomas . . . ' It was Rose's voice but to Fury she sounded dreamy. The way she had said his name seemed to last forever, to go on and on.

'Thooooooooooooommmmmmaaaaa-asssss.'

'Rose,' Fury said. 'Rose!'

'Hush,' Rose said and then she was kneeling beside her husband, a soothing hand upon his forehead. 'Don't speak. Don't say anything.'

Fury looked up into her eyes; like glistening pools, the eyes were inviting him in to the warmth of the water.

'Rose,' Fury said. 'I've missed you, Rose. Every single day I've thought of you.'

'I know,' she said and bent closer so that she could kiss him. And when she did, the touch of her lips upon his forehead vanquished the pain that had ebbed through his body.

'I love you, Rose,' Fury said. 'I love you so much.'

'I love you too,' Rose said. 'Now hush. It is not your time. Not yet.'

And then there was blackness and the warmth Fury felt was replaced with a bone-numbing cold. He gritted his teeth against a fresh wave of pain as once more his side seemed to explode.

And then he was looking through an opaque shroud and he saw another face shimmering into view.

'Rose,' he whispered.

But it wasn't Rose.

It was the face of Bina.

'Keep still,' she said, which confused Fury.

'Rose . . . ' Fury said, hearing his own words fade away into nothing. 'Rose.'

Then blackness before once again his wife was beside him, smiling down at him, lights cascading within her eyes.

'Rose,' Fury said again and smiled. 'I want to stay with you. I don't want to go.'

Rose smiled, shook her head, said, 'No. It is not yet time.'

'Yes,' Fury said. 'I want to be with you again.'

'You shall,' Rose said. 'Though not yet.'

Once more Rose vanished, taking all

the warmth with her and Fury again felt the agony that was racking his entire body. He tried to hold a scream that was forming on his lips, but the pain was too great and he screamed at the top of his voice, almost choking as warm blood bubbled in his mouth.

'Rose . . . ' he whispered, the words almost inaudible, gossamer-thin on his lips. 'Don't go, Rose.'

19

It had been more than five months since Marlow had received word that Fury was dead, killed by Haw Tabor who had in turn been killed by an Indian girl brandishing a sawn-down shotgun.

The rancher would have preferred it had there been a body, but Fury had been carried off by two young Indians and had vanished. The reports were that Fury had been gut shot and would not survive the wounds — could not survive the wounds.

Nevertheless for a time Marlow had been expecting Fury to turn up, still breathing, guns still spitting vengeance. For weeks following the reports of Fury's shooting, Marlow had lived on his nerves. And it was only recently that the rancher had started to relax, coming to the conclusion that Fury was indeed dead. He had no idea of the identity of the two Indians who had spirited away his body, nor did he really care.

It was enough that Fury was dead and that this was finally over.

Marlow lit one of his cigars and smiled, thinking that he owed the Indians, whoever they were, a great debt. After all it was one of them, a girl apparently, who had gunned down Haw Tabor, thus saving Marlow a sizable sum of blood money.

He crossed the room and went to the window, peering out into the darkness. All seemed deathly quiet out there, just the way Marlow liked it. He stood there for some time, smoking his cigar and thinking of Fury.

The man had gotten very close before Haw Tabor had gunned him down, ending up dead himself for his troubles. Fury had been barely alive when the two Indians had taken him, least that was what Marlow had heard, and everyone who had been there, everyone who Marlow had spoken to, had said there was no way Fury could have survived, he had been too badly injured.

It had been three days after the shoot-out at Carver's Crossing that news had first come to Marlow, and he had left his foreman, Ned Rawlings, in charge of the ranch and ridden out together with Sheriff Hoskins and a small army of well-armed men.

Marlow had seen Haw Tabor's body, together with the other men Fury had killed at Carver's Crossing, and he had paid a couple of men to bury the gunman outside the town.

Marlow and his men had then ridden out, scouring the countryside for any sign of Fury and the two Indians, but there had been nothing. Initially they had been able to pick up on tracks. They followed these tracks for several miles but eventually they had disappeared. It seemed that the Indians, whoever they had been, had spirited Fury away somewhere he would never be found.

Eventually Marlow had returned to the ranch and for some weeks the place was kept on high alert, guards remained posted at strategic points around the valley that surrounded the ranch house. Though the weeks turned into months and gradually Marlow started to believe that Fury was indeed dead, that there was no way he could have escaped the injuries visited him by the now-dead gunman Haw Tabor.

Marlow drained his whiskey, went to the cabinet and poured himself another before returning to his chair and once again gazing out of the window. He wondered for how much longer Thomas Fury would occupy his thoughts. And although the rancher had stopped worrying that the man was still alive, had convinced himself that he was dead, there was still not a day that went by without him thinking of Thomas Fury.

There was a knock on the door and Marlow turned, shouted for the caller to enter.

'Father.' Ellie stuck her head around the door before coming into the room. 'Are you all right, Father?'

'I'm fine,' Marlow said and smiled warmly at his daughter, thinking how beautiful she was. She was turning into a fine woman. 'I'm just enjoying a cigar and a whiskey.'

'You enjoy that whiskey a little too much,' she gently chided.

'You know,' Marlow said and sipped from the glass, 'I think you may be right there. Don't worry, I'll make this my last one.'

'Promise?'

'I promise,' Marlow said.

Ellie smiled, said, 'I'm going to bed. You should too. It's late.'

Marlow smiled at his daughter, took another gulp of his whiskey.

'I'll be retiring soon enough,' he said. 'Just finish this drink and my cigar first.'

'Don't leave it too late,' Ellie said and closed the door.

Marlow smiled, drained his whiskey,

crossed the room to the cabinet and poured himself yet another. He'd promised his daughter he wouldn't have another but the rancher felt in need of just one last drink.

'This is the last one, I promise,' he said and held the glass up as if saluting the room.

He went and sat back in the chair besides the window, drew upon his cigar and took a gentle sip of the amber-coloured liquid.

It tasted good and he felt all the tension escaping from his weary frame.

20

Fury had ground-tied his horse some ways back and covered the last half mile to Marlow's ranch on foot. He felt the odd twinge in his side but he figured he should be grateful that's all it was. The Colt Paterson wielded by Haw Tabor had very nearly killed him; indeed he'd been incredibly lucky to survive. The bullet had entered his body on the left side, just below the rib cage and passed straight through him. He'd lost a lot of blood but other than a couple of broken ribs, there had been very little internal damage.

Bina and Rake had gotten him away from Carver's Crossing, tied him to a horse and ridden like crazy until they had reached the wagon they had left behind. Then they had transferred Fury, who by this point was feverish and close to death, to the wagon and taken him up into the hills where Bina had treated him with skills learned from her people. She had dressed his wounds, pushing yarrow leaves into the hole in his side and bathed the wound daily. She had used snakeweed to break Fury's fever and gradually, over a period of weeks he had begun to heal. During this period Rake had proved himself a good hunter and daily Fury had been fed on soups made from desert rabbit, wild turkey and the liver of mountain lion.

Slowly but surely, Fury's strength had returned and barely ten days after he had been shot he had managed to get to his feet and take a few steps. Of course he had been weak, at first his legs could hardly support him. He had lost a lot of weight and every time he moved he felt a searing pain in his side. The wound had left behind an ugly scar, an indentation where Fury had lost a sizeable chunk of flesh, but he figured he had gotten off lightly and the Colt Paterson could have done a hell of a lot more damage. Indeed, had Bina not shot him down then Fury had no doubt that the gunman would have finished him off.

There was no question of that.

Marlow's ranch house had been built using the natural defences of the valley walls and as Fury approached the valley, he was cautious. It was a dark night, with little if any illumination provided by the pale moon that hung suspended in an overcast sky and visibility was poor, making it difficult to see if anyone was about.

Still, Fury figured, if it made it difficult for him to see then it would also make it harder for any guards Marlow had posted about the place to see him.

If he was careful he might just make the ranch house without alerting anyone to his presence.

He entered the valley; keeping his back to the wall, he slowly made his way across. He had gone some way when he heard movement ahead of him and he immediately cleared leather and crouched down. Fury remained like that for several moments, slowing his breathing while he tried to pick out further sounds, but there was nothing.

Only silence.

Earlier today Fury had left Bina and Rake, saying his farewells and wishing them well.

The two young Indians had accepted that the time to go their separate ways had arrived and they didn't even try to talk Fury out of going after the Marlow boy.

There would be no changing Fury's mind.

He had sworn to gain vengeance on those who had killed his wife and unborn child: Luke Marlow was the last of those men left alive.

When that was done, Fury had said, then and only then would he be free to move on, but not before.

No, not before he finished this.

For a moment Fury thought of the

two young people who had shared his life these last few months. They had planned to ride out until they found somewhere to settle, to build a life for themselves. During their time together they had fallen in love, that much was obvious and Fury took heart from that. It was the one good thing that had come out of this situation.

A sound again.

Once again Fury crouched and stared into the darkness.

Gradually he saw something, a shape in the darkness, more shadow than substance, almost a shifting of black on black; he edged closer until the vague shape of a man became visible. The man had his back to Fury and was concentrating on the quirly he was smoking.

Fury would prefer not to kill the man.

Luke Marlow had to die but if it were at all possible, Fury would rather avoid further bloodshed.

He decided his best option was to

move forward quickly, take the man by surprise and silence him before the alarm was raised.

Fury took a deep breath and pounced, bringing the butt of his gun down hard on the back of the man's neck, knocking him into unconsciousness.

Fury crouched over the man. He would be all right, but would have an almighty headache when he came around. Fury removed the man's gun belt, unwound the lace that ran through the leather and used it to firmly bind his hands behind his back. Next, he removed the man's bandana and used it as a gag, stuffing part of it into his mouth and then tying it tightly behind his head.

He dragged the still-unconscious man over to the valley wall and left him there, figuring it would be some time before he came around.

Then Fury continued further into the valley and eventually he saw the thin glow of a light in one of the windows of the ranch house. There was a bunkhouse directly opposite the ranch house; suddenly the door swung open, a man came out and stretched himself before crossing to a smaller building, which Fury guessed served as a privy for the ranch hands.

Crouching once more, Fury waited for what seemed an age for the man to emerge from the privy and make his way back to the bunkhouse.

Now Fury approached the ranch house, stepped up onto the boardwalk and reached for the door handle. He tried it, twisting it slowly and found that it was not locked.

He silently pushed the door open and then stepped inside, closing the door behind him.

Inside Fury stood still, once again having to allow his eyes to adjust to the gloom. There was a door ahead of him and to the left. He could see the faint glow of candlelight flickering around the frame.

He made his way slowly towards it and once again turned the handle.

Fury opened the door and stepped inside a room that looked like some kind of office. He immediately drew his eyes to the figure slumbering in the chair by the window. The man had a half drunk glass of whiskey in one hand and a cigar that had long burnt out in the other.

Fury knew this was Dan Marlow, father of Luke Marlow.

Walking on feet that felt like they were made of lead, Fury quickly and quietly stepped out of the room and silently closed the door behind him. He waited for a moment until he was sure Marlow hadn't woken and then he checked all the other rooms on the lower floor, each time silently opening and closing doors and found that all the rooms were empty.

Fury found the stairs and slowly made his way up.

There were four rooms on the upper floor. Fury guessed they were all bedrooms; he went to the closest and silently turned the door handle.

He pushed the door open and stepped inside.

And looked down at the figure of Luke Marlow in the bed.

The figure in the bed was carrying a lot of weight, his face looked so bloated that his cheeks were puffed up.

The man had put on bulk since the last time Fury had seen him but this was Luke Marlow.

There was no mistaking those cold eyes.

Fury raised his gun and pointed it squarely at the man in the bed.

It was only then that Fury realised that Luke was awake and staring back at him, a curious look upon his face.

A vacant look.

He ain't seeing me, Fury thought.

He crossed the room and went to the bed, grabbed Luke Marlow by the throat and peered deep into his eyes, but there was no change in the man's expression. The man simply stared back at Fury but didn't appear to be seeing him and there was no change at all as

Fury tightened his grip on the man's throat. The man might as well have been a rag doll.

'You're dead already,' Fury said, as he suddenly realised all this had been for nothing. Luke Marlow was lying in that bed, still breathing, technically alive but to all intents and purposes the man was already dead.

No, not dead.

This was worse than death.

Fury had seen men like this before and whether it had been an illness or an accident that had brought Luke Marlow to this condition, there would never be a recovery. That much was obvious from the total lack of response in the man. Fury had come all this way to seek vengeance on Luke Marlow and yet the man who had violated and killed his wife no longer existed, replaced instead by this human vegetable.

This shell.

A living dead man.

'Can you hear me?' Fury asked and

for a moment he was sure he saw some kind of recognition in the man's eyes — an almost imperceptible dilating of the irises perhaps, but other than that nothing. 'I ain't going to kill you. You're already dead.'

Fury released his hold on the man's throat and saw there was no reaction at all.

He could have throttled the man here and now and there wouldn't have been any reaction.

'I ain't going to kill you,' Fury said again.

'I'm glad to hear it.'

The words came from behind and Fury spun, his gun at the ready, and looked on the features of a beautiful young woman. She stood there in the doorway, dressed only in a flowing nightdress.

'I'm Ellie Marlow,' she said. 'That man there used to be my brother, Luke.'

Fury looked at the woman, said nothing.

'He was kicked in the head by a horse,' the woman explained. 'Ain't been right since and the doctor's say he never will be again. My father . . . ' her face suddenly clouded over, as if she had just realised something.

'Your father's sleeping downstairs,' Fury said. 'I ain't harmed him none and I figure it's best he stay that way.'

The woman smiled, nodded, asked, 'So what are you going to do now?'

'I came to kill him,' Fury pointed to the empty shell on the bed. 'But I guess he's already dead.'

'You're Thomas Fury?' the woman said.

'I am,' Fury replied.

'We thought you were dead.'

Fury turned back to look at Luke Marlow, thinking that maybe his own soul was just as inert as the man laying in the bed.

'Maybe I am,' Fury said. 'Maybe I am.'

'Sometimes I think death would be a mercy for Luke,' the woman said.

Again, Fury looked long and hard at Luke Marlow before turning back to the woman.

'I don't owe him no mercy,' he said and holstered his gun.

The woman said nothing and stood there as Fury pushed past her and went back out into the night.

It was over.

It was finally over.

We do hope that you have enjoyed reading this large print book.

Did you know that all of our titles are available for purchase?

We publish a wide range of high quality large print books including:
Romances, Mysteries, Classics
General Fiction
Non Fiction and Westerns

Special interest titles available in large print are:
The Little Oxford Dictionary
Music Book, Song Book
Hymn Book, Service Book

Also available from us courtesy of Oxford University Press:
Young Readers' Dictionary
(large print edition)
Young Readers' Thesaurus
(large print edition)

For further information or a free brochure, please contact us at:
Ulverscroft Large Print Books Ltd.,
The Green, Bradgate Road, Anstey,
Leicester, LE7 7FU, England.
Tel: (00 44) **0116 236 4325**
Fax: (00 44) **0116 234 0205**

HARD STONE

James Clay

When range detective Rance Dehner kills outlaw Tully Brooks, he finds that the case will not be closed so easily. Before dying, Brooks tells Dehner that he was involved in a fake bank robbery, and an innocent man has been arrested for the hold-up; his dying request is that Dehner investigate. The detective's compliance sends him to Hard Stone, Colorado, where he must deal with a high-stakes gambler, a mining engineer who's always quick to draw his gun, and a mysterious assailant who seems determined to ambush and kill him . . .

THE GAMBLER AND THE LAW

Will DuRey

Blamed for the murder of a prominent politician, gambler Dan Freemont is forced to flee Nebraska. Pursued by the real killer's henchmen, he arrives at the small Wyoming town of Beecher Gulch, where he hopes a planned rendezvous with a US marshal will prove his innocence. But a conflict is developing between the settlers and Carl Benton, the cattle king of the territory. Mistaken for a town-taming lawman brought in to oppose the cattlemen, Dan is soon involved in the dispute, and becomes a target for Benton's gunmen . . .

BLOOD WILL HAVE BLOOD

Lee Lejeune

The peaceful town of Silver Spur is horrified when the Holby family is murdered, and suspicion immediately falls upon a stranger who had recently been in town asking for directions to the Holby farm. Sheriff Jack Kincade tracks the man to a neighbouring town and discovers he is Snake Holby, the murdered man's brother. Then a local boy tells the sheriff that he overheard three men talking about how they had massacred the family as an act of revenge. Jack and Snake set out to discover the culprits . . .

FIGHTING RANGER

Corba Sunman

Travis Logan, a Texas Ranger, is heading for Alder Creek when big trouble comes over a ridge, in the shape of a woman being chased by two killers. Pledged to fight lawlessness, Logan goes into action, and is engulfed by the trouble he searches out. The odds are greatly stacked against him; and when hot lead starts flying, they won't improve until Logan untangles a web of deceit, and stamps his particular brand of law and order on the greedy, callous men who stand in his way . . .